30

Marc Reklau is a coach, speaker and a bestselling author. Marc's mission is to empower people to create the life they want and to give them the resources and tools to make it happen.

His message is simple: Many people want to change things in their lives, but few are willing to do a simple set of exercises constantly over a period of time. You can plan and create success and happiness in your life by installing habits that support you on the way to your goals.

If you want to work with Marc, directly contact him on his homepage www.marcreklau.com, where you can also find more information about him.

You can connect with him on Twitter @MarcReklau, Facebook or on his website www.goodhabitsacademy.com.

30 DAYS
Change your habits,
Change your life

MARC REKLAU

RUPA

Published by
Rupa Publications India Pvt. Ltd 2019
7/16, Ansari Road, Daryaganj
New Delhi 110002

Sales centres:
Bengaluru Chennai
Hyderabad Jaipur Kathmandu
Kolkata Mumbai Prayagraj

P-ISBN: 978-93-5333-520-5
E-ISBN: 978-93-5333-521-2

Twenty-fifth impression 2023

30 29 28 27 26 25

The moral right of the author has been asserted.

Printed in India

Disclaimer

This book is designed to provide information and motivation to our readers. It is sold with the understanding that the publisher is not engaged to render any type of psychological, legal or any other kind of professional advice. The instructions and advice in this book are not intended as a substitute for counseling. The content of each chapter is the sole expression and opinion of its author. No warranties or guarantees are expressed or implied by the author's and publisher's choice to include any of the content in this volume. Neither the publisher nor the individual author shall be liable for any physical, psychological, emotional, financial or commercial damages, including, but not limited to, special, incidental, consequential or other damages. Our views and rights are the same:

You must test everything for yourself according to your own situation, talents and aspirations.

You are responsible for your own decisions, choices, actions and results.

The beginning is the most important part of the work.

—PLATO

Contents

Introduction

If you think you can, you're right,
if you think you can't, you're right.

—HENRY FORD

Look around you. What do you see? Look at your surroundings, the atmosphere and the people around you. Think of your current life conditions: work, health, friends, people surrounding you. What do they look like? Are you happy with what you see? Now look inside of you. How do you feel RIGHT NOW in this moment? Are you satisfied with your life? Are you longing for more? Do you believe that you can be happy and successful? What is missing from your life that you need to make it happy and/or successful? Why do some people seem to have everything and other people nothing? Most people have no idea how they get what they get. Some of us just blame it on fate and chance. I'm sorry that I have to be the one to tell you: "Sorry, friend! You have created the life you have! Everything that happens to you is created by YOU—either consciously by design or unconsciously by default; it's not a result of fate or circumstances.

I decided to write this book because I'm seeing so many people that are dreaming of improving their life, being happier, becoming wealthier yet according to them, the only way that could happen would be due to some kind of miracle: winning the lottery, marrying rich or some other stroke of luck. They are looking for outside influences to happen by chance and change everything. They think life happens to them. Most of them have no idea that they can be in total control of their life each and every moment and every day of their lives. So, they continue daydreaming, doing those things that they've always done, and waiting for some miraculous outcome. Sometimes, they actually don't even know what they want! The following is a conversation I actually had:

Q: "What would you do if you had enough time and money?"

A: "Man! That would be great! I would be happy!"

Q: "And what would 'being happy' look like to you?"

A: "I would do everything I want to do!"

Q: "And what is 'everything you want to do'?"

A: "Oh! Now you got me. I don't even know!"

The true tragedy is that if they would only stop for one moment, ask themselves what **they really want in life**, write down their goals and start working toward them, they could actually make those miracles happen. I see it day in and day out with my coaching clients: people that come to me because they want to change something in their lives, and instead of sitting around and waiting and dreaming of a better life, they actually take matters in their own hands and start taking action! And the results are fabulous!

Remember: You are leading the life that you have chosen! How? This is because we create our life every moment through our thoughts, beliefs and expectations and our mind is so powerful that it will give us what we ask for. The good thing is that you can train your mind to give you only the things you want, and not the things that you don't want! And it gets even better: you can learn how to deal with things that you can't control in a more efficient and less painful manner.

I've been studying the principles of success and how to achieve happiness for nearly 25 years now. What I always subconsciously knew became a structured method using the tools and exercises of coaching. More than ever, I'm convinced that success can be planned and created. For the skeptics who think that all this is metaphysical nonsense, just look at the enormous progress science has made and how it can now prove many things which only 25 years ago could only be believed without being proven. The most important message in this little book is: **Your happiness depends of YOU, and nobody else!** In this book, I want to introduce you to some proven tips, tricks and exercises that can improve your life beyond your imagination **if you practise them constantly and persistently**. More good news: You don't need to win the lottery to be happy! You can start by doing little things in your life differently in a constant and consistent manner, and over time, results will show. This is how my coaching clients achieve incredible results: creating new habits and working toward their goals consistently, and doing things that bring them closer to their goals every single day. **It is possible! You can do it! You deserve it!**

Simply reading the book won't help you a lot, though. You have to take ACTION! That's the most important part—(and it is also the part that I struggled with the most for many, many years). **You have to start doing and practising the exercises and introducing new habits into your life.** If you are very curious—read the whole book once with a pen or pencil and a notebook in hand to make notes if you like. Then read the book a second time—this is when the rubber meets the road— and now start doing some of the exercises and introducing new habits into your life. If you do the exercises in this book regularly and consistently, your life will change for the better! Experts in the field of success teachings, coaching and Neurolinguistic Programming agree that it takes 21 to 30 days to implement a new habit; 30 days that can make a difference in your life. 30 days of working consistently on yourself and your habits can turn it all around—or at least put you in a better position. At least try it out! Stay with some of the exercises for at least 30 days. Do the ones that come easy to you. If it doesn't work out for you, write me an email with your complaint to *marc@ marcreklau.com*

I have also provided some WORKSHEETS on my homepage. Download them and **HAVE FUN!**

1

Rewrite your story

*Change the way you look at things
and the things you look at change.*

—WAYNE W. DYER

The first time I came in contact with this idea was nearly 25 years ago while reading Jane Roberts's book "Seth Speaks". Seth says **you are the writer, director and main actor of your story.** So if you don't like how the story is playing out...change it! At that time, I thought it's kind of a comforting idea, gave it a try, and have lived by it ever since—in good times and bad times. **It doesn't matter what happened in your past. Your future is a clean sheet!** You can reinvent yourself! Every day brings with it the opportunity to start a new life! You get to choose your identity at each and every moment! So who are you going to be? It's up to you to decide who you are going to be from this day on. What are you going to do?

If you DO some of the things suggested in this book, create new habits, and do just some of the many exercises that you will find here, things will start to shift. **It's not going to be**

easy and you will need discipline, patience and persistence. But the results will come.

In 2008, when FC Barcelona's coach Josep "Pep" Guardiola took charge of the team that was in a desolate state, he told the 73,000 people in attendance in the stadium and the millions of viewers on Catalonian television, in his inauguration speech: "We can't promise you titles, what we can promise you is effort and that we will persist, persist, persist until the end. Fasten your seatbelts—we are going to have fun." This speech started the most successful period in the 115 years history of the club and few people think it can ever be repeated. The team went on to win three national championships, two national cups, three Spanish Supercups, two European Supercups, two Champions Leagues and two World Club Championships in their four years of domination of World football. (If you don't follow soccer: This is like a mediocre NFL team winning four Superbowls in a row).

They rewrote their story.

Now it's your turn. Make some effort and persist, persist, persist! Don't give up! Fasten your seatbelts and have some fun!

2

Self-discipline and commitment

It was character that got us out of bed, commitment that moved us into action and discipline that enabled us to follow through.

—ZIG ZIGLAR

If you cannot do great things, do small things in a great way.

—NAPOLEON HILL

This is one of the first chapters because it will be the foundation of your future success. Your way to success and happiness is deeply connected to your willpower and commitment. These character traits will decide whether you do what you said you would do and go through with it. These will keep you going toward your goals, even when everything seems to go against you. **Self-discipline is doing the things you need to do, even if you are not in the mood for it.** If you train to be self-disciplined and have the will to succeed, you can do great things in your life. But even if you don't have the slightest bit of self-discipline within you right now, don't worry. You can start training your self-discipline and willpower from this moment on! Self-discipline is like a muscle. The more you train it, the better you get. If your self-discipline is weak right now, start training it by setting yourself small, reachable goals. Write down the success you have and keep in mind that you don't have limits—only the ones you set for yourself.

Visualize the benefits you will have at the end of the road: For example, if you want to go running at 6 a.m. in the morning and you just don't seem to make it out of bed—imagine how good you will feel when you are at the fitness level that you want to be at and how great you will look. Then jump out of bed, put on your running clothes, and go! Remember: **This book will only work if you have the will and the discipline to make it work!**

What is your word worth? Take your commitments seriously! Because not keeping your commitments has a terrible consequence: you lose energy, you lose clarity, you get confused along the way to your goals, and even worse, you lose self-confidence, and your self-esteem takes a hit! To avoid this, you have to become aware of what is really important to you and act in line with your values.

A commitment is a choice! Only make commitments that you really want. That can mean fewer commitments and more "NOs". If you commit, keep your commitment—whatever it takes. Give them the importance and value that they deserve and be aware of the consequences of not keeping them.

Time to take action!

Ask yourself the following questions:

In what areas are you lacking self-discipline at the moment? Be completely honest.

What benefits will you obtain if you had more self-discipline?

What will be your first step toward reaching your goal?

Write down your plan of action in small steps. Give yourself deadlines.

How will you know you've reached your goal of having more self-discipline in _____?

3

Take full responsibility for your life

*Peak performance begins with your taking
complete responsibility for your life and
everything that happens to you.*

—BRIAN TRACY

*Most people do not really want freedom,
because freedom involves responsibility, and
most people are frightened of responsibility.*

—SIGMUND FREUD

There is only one person that's responsible for your life and
that is YOU! Not your boss, not your spouse, not your parents,
not your friends, not your clients, not the economy, not the
weather. YOU! The day we stop blaming others for everything
that happens in our life, everything changes! Taking responsibility
for your life is taking charge of your life and becoming the
protagonist of it. Instead of being a victim of circumstances,
you obtain the power to create your own circumstances or at
least the power to decide how you are going to act in the face

of circumstances that life presents to you. It doesn't matter what happens to you in your life; it matters what attitude you adopt. And the attitude you adopt is your choice!

If you blame your life situation on others, what has to happen to make your life better? All of the others have to change! And that, my friend, I tell you, is not going to happen. If you are the protagonist, YOU have the power to change the things that you don't like in your life! You are in control of your thoughts, actions and feelings. You are in control of your words, the series you watch on TV, and the people you spend your time with. If you don't like your results, change your input—your thoughts, emotions and expectations. Stop reacting to others and start responding. Reaction is automatic. Responding is consciously choosing your response.

You take your life in your own hands, and what happens?
A terrible thing: no one to blame

—ERICA JONG

The victim says: Every bad thing in my life is others' fault, but **if you are not part of the problem, then you also can't be a part of the solution.** Or, in other words, if the problem is caused by the outside, the solution is also on the outside. If you're coming in late to work because of "traffic", what has to happen so that you can get to work on time? Traffic has to disappear magically! Because as long as there is traffic, you will always be late. Or you can act like a protagonist and leave home on time. Then it depends on you.

So once again: even if you don't have control over the stimuli that environment sends you continuously, you have the liberty to choose your behavior in facing the situation.

The person with a "victim mentality" only reacts, is always innocent, and constantly blames others for his or her life situation, while using the past as justification and putting their hopes on a future which will miraculously bring solutions to problems or a change in others who are causing the troubles.

The protagonist knows that he or she is responsible, chooses adequate behavior and holds himself accountable. He uses the past as a valuable experience from which to learn, lives in the present where he sees constant opportunities for change, and decides and goes after his future goals. The most important question is: "Who will you choose to be—by your actions—when life presents you with these circumstances?"

Gandhi said it very nicely: "They can't take away our self-respect if we don't give it to them."

Ask yourself the following questions:

Who are you blaming for your life situation right now? (Your partner? Your boss? Your parents? Your friends?)

What would happen if you stopped blaming the others for what happens to you in your life?

What would happen if you would stop being a victim of the circumstances?

Is it comfortable for you being the victim?

What benefits does it have for you to be a victim?

What would happen if you stopped suffering in your life and took the decision to change it?

What would you change?

Where could you start?

How would you start?

Action Step:

Write down 5 things that you can do in the coming week to start changing the course and start taking charge of your life.

4

Choices and decisions

*Once you make a decision, the universe
conspires to make it happen.*

—RALPH WALDO EMERSON

Maybe you have heard that your life is the result of the decisions you made. How do you feel about that? Is this true for you? It's important that from now on, you are aware of the power you have over your life by making decisions! Every decision, every choice has an important influence on your life. In fact, your life is a direct result of the choices and decisions you made in the past and every choice carries a consequence. Start making better choices. **Remember that you choose your thoughts and even your feelings.**

The most important thing is to take decisions. Whether the decision is right or wrong is secondary. You will soon receive feedback that will help you to progress. Once you have made a decision, go with it and take the consequences. If it was wrong, learn from it and forgive yourself knowing that at that point in time and with the knowledge you had, it was the best and the right decision to take.

YOUR ATTITUDE + YOUR DECISIONS = YOUR LIFE

Viktor Frankl was a Jewish psychologist imprisoned in Germany's concentration camps during the Second World War. He lost his entire family, except his sister. Under these terrible circumstances, he became aware of what he named "the ultimate human freedom", which not even the Nazi prison wards could take away from him: they could control his external circumstances, **but in the last instance, it was him who CHOSE HOW these circumstances were going to affect him!**

He found out that between STIMULUS and RESPONSE there was a small space in time in which he had the freedom to CHOOSE his RESPONSE! This means that even if you may not be able to control the circumstances that life presents to you, you can always **choose** your response in facing those circumstances, and by doing so have a huge impact on your life.

In other words, what hurts us is not what happens to us, but our response to what happens to us. The most important thing is how we RESPOND to what happens to us in our lives. And that is a CHOICE!

Do you want to be healthier? Make better choices about food and exercise. Do you want to be more successful? Make better decisions about who you surround yourself with, what you read and what you watch. There are no excuses!

Forgive me if I make the assumption that your life situation is not worse than Viktor Frankl's when he made this discovery: for me being a Jew in a German concentration camp in World War II is as bad as it gets.

Ask yourself the following questions:

What decisions could you take today to start change?

Will you choose to be more flexible? More positive? Healthier? Happier?

Action Steps:

1) Write down at least three changes that you want to make today:
   i) _____
   ii) _____
   iii) _____
2) Read Viktor Frankl's book "Man's Search for Meaning".

5

Choose your thoughts

*The universe is change; our life is
what our thoughts make it.*

—MARCUS AURELIUS

*You are today where your thoughts have
brought you; you will be tomorrow where
your thoughts take you.*

—JAMES ALLEN

If you want to improve your life, the first thing you have to do is improve your thoughts. Your thoughts create your reality so you better have them under control! By controlling your thoughts, ultimately you control your life and your destiny. So observe your thoughts every now and then. Peace Pilgrim's quote, "If you realized how powerful your thoughts are, you would never think a negative thought," says it all. Don't get stuck in negative thoughts. Replace them with positive thoughts, such as "everything is going to be all right"—every single time they come up.

Think positive! A positively thinking person is not a dreamer, who thinks there are no problems in life. Instead, he or she recognizes that problems are opportunities to grow, and knows that they only have the meaning that they are given. **Positive thinking is to see the reality as it is, accept it, and make the best of it.** Don't let your thoughts dominate you, instead dominate your thoughts and control their quality. Train your mind to concentrate only on positive, creative, and inspiring thoughts. If you train your mind like this for a while, you will see that the circumstances of your life change too. You are the creator of your thoughts, but you are not your thoughts. Your thoughts are energy and the energy follows the thought. Thoughts create emotions, which create behavior, which create actions, and those actions have consequences in your daily life.

THOUGHT EMOTION BEHAVIOR ACTION

Your thoughts depend on your beliefs about life. If you don't like what you are receiving, then have a look at what you are sending! Everything that is in your life has been created by your thoughts, expectations and beliefs. So analyze them! If you change your beliefs, you will get new results!

Practise a thought often enough so that it becomes a belief, and your behavior and actions will follow its lead. For instance, if you constantly worry about not having enough money, you'll create behaviors based on fear. You'll play smaller. You'll try to hang on to the money you have versus playing to win.

Action Step:

Try to have no negative thoughts for 48 hours. Block them from the first moment and substitute them with positive thoughts of love, peace and compassion. Even if it seems difficult at the beginning, hang in there. It gets easier. Then try this for 5 days, and finally a week. What has changed in your life since you started thinking positively?

6
What do you believe?

These then are my last words to you.
Be not afraid of life. Believe that life is worth
living and your belief will help create the fact.

—WILLIAM JAMES

The outer conditions of a person's life will always
be found to reflect their inner beliefs.

—JAMES ALLEN

What do you believe? This is extremely important, because ultimately your beliefs create your reality! You create what you believe and your world is only your interpretation of the reality. In other words, we don't see the world how it is, but how we were conditioned to see it. Our perception is only an approximation of reality. Our maps of the reality determine the way we act more than the reality itself. Each **one of us sees the world through the lenses of their own beliefs.** Does this sound like hocus-pocus to you? It did to me too until I studied two semesters of Psychology at my High School and learned about the **Placebo Effect, The Pygmalion Effect, and Self-Fulfilling prophecies**. Studies on these subjects out there show how powerful our thoughts and beliefs really are! But what is a belief? It's the conscious and unconscious information that we accept as true. Robert Dilts defines beliefs as judgments and assessments about ourselves, others, and the world around us. A belief is a habitual thought pattern. Once a person believes something is true (whether it's true or not), he or she acts as if it were—collecting facts to prove the belief even if it's false.

Beliefs are like a self-fulfilling prophecy. They work like this: **your beliefs influence your emotions, your emotions influence your actions and your actions influence your RESULTS!** Depending on your belief system, you live your life one way or another.

I want you to realize that life doesn't just happen to you! It's a reflection of your beliefs, thoughts, and expectations. If you want to change your life, you have to first change your patterns of thinking.

Even if beliefs come from early childhood programming for most of us, we are able to change them. **Nobody can impose your beliefs on you.** It's always you who in the last instance can permit a belief to be true for you or not! Believing in yourself is an attitude. It's a choice! Remember what Henry Ford said! If you think that you won't make it, if you think that it's impossible, then you will not achieve it, even if your effort is huge. For many decades, it was thought impossible that man could run a mile under four minutes. There were even scientific papers and studies on the subject. These studies could all be shredded on 6 May 1954, when Roger Bannister proved everybody wrong at a race in Oxford. From then on, over a 1,000 people have done it.

I highly recommend that you let go of limiting beliefs, such as:

- One can't be totally happy, as there is always something that goes wrong.
- Life is tough.
- Showing emotions is for weak people.
- Opportunity only knocks once.
- I'm helpless and have no control over my life.
- I don't deserve it.
- Nobody loves me.
- I can't.
- It's impossible.
- ....

And pick up some empowering beliefs, such as:

- I create my destiny.
- Nobody can hurt me if I don't allow it.
- Life is great!
- Everything happens for a reason.
- Everything is going to be all right.
- I can do it!

Ask yourself the following questions:

What do I believe to be true about myself?

What are my beliefs concerning money?

What are my beliefs concerning my relationships?

What are my beliefs about my body?

To change a belief follow this exercise and say to yourself:

1) This is only my belief about the reality. That doesn't mean that it is the reality.
2) Although I believe this, it's not necessarily true.
3) Create emotions which are opposite to the belief.
4) Imagine the opposite.
5) Be aware that the belief is only an idea that you have about reality and not reality itself.
6) For just 10 minutes a day, ignore what seems to be real and act as if your wish has come true. (See yourself spending money, being healthy, more successful, etc.)

Alternative exercise:

1) Write down the limiting belief.
2) Remember the sequence: belief—emotion—action—result.
3) To get a different result, in what way do you need to act?
4) How do you need to feel in order to act differently and get a different result?
5) What do you need to believe in order to feel differently, act differently and get a different result?

7

The importance of your attitude

Everything can be taken from a man but one thing:
the last of human freedoms—to choose one's attitude
in any given set of circumstances.

—VIKTOR FRANKL

Your Attitude is crucial for your happiness! It can change your way of seeing things dramatically and also your way of facing them. You will suffer less in life if you accept the rules of the game. Life is made up of laughter and tears, light and shadow. You have to accept the bad moments by changing your way of looking at them. Everything that happens to you is a challenge and an opportunity at the same time.

Look at the positive side of things in life, even in the worst situations. There is something good hidden in every bad— although sometimes, it might take some time to discover it.

I'll tell you again: it's not what happens in your life that's important; it's how you respond to what happens to you that makes your life! Life is a chain of moments—some happy, some sad—and it depends on you to make the best of each and every one of those moments. Did your wife leave you? So will you be unhappy forever or will you go out and meet new people? Losing your job might open new doors.

Many years ago all of the success teachers and positive thinkers described it this way: "If life gives you a lemon, add sugar to it, and make lemonade out of it". Younger readers might say that "If life gives you a lemon, ask for some salt and Tequila". You get the point, don't you?

For example, some healthy attitudes are:

- Allow yourself to make mistakes and learn from them.
- Admit that there are things you don't know.
- Dare asking for help and let other people help you.
- Differentiate between what you have done in your life until now and what you want to do or better still, will do from now on!

Action Step:

Think of a negative situation and turn it around.

8

Perspective is everything

The optimist sees the donut,
the pessimist sees the hole.

—OSCAR WILDE

A pessimist is somebody who complains about
the noise when opportunity knocks.

—OSCAR WILDE

William Shakespeare said, "There is nothing either good or bad, but thinking makes it so." Put things into perspective! The closer you are to the problem and the more in front of it, the less you see. Step back and get a more global view of it. Understand how you feel faced with the problem and evaluate the real importance of it. Even seeing the problem as a challenge will be helpful! Every negative experience in your life has something good in it—search for it! If you get into the habit of always searching for the good in every situation, you will change the quality of your life drastically.

Experiences themselves are neutral until we start to give

them meaning. Your vision of the world and your perspective "decide" if something is "good" or "bad". What may be a great tragedy to you could be a wake-up call for me to take my life into my hands and thrive. In coaching, we use what is called "Reframing" to change the perspective that a client has of an event. One of my favorites is changing "Failure" to "Feedback" or "Learning experience".

How do you feel if you say, **"I failed terribly in my last relationship"?** Now try saying, **"I learned so much from my last relationship, I'm sure I will not make the same mistakes again!"** Can you feel the difference? Here are some more examples of reframing:

Action Step:

Write down at least 5 situations in your life that you thought were negative; however, with time you clearly saw that you got something good out of it.

9

Have patience and never ever give up!

Our greatest weakness lies in giving up.
The most certain way to succeed is always to
try just one more time.

—THOMAS ALVA EDISON

Success is not final, failure is not fatal:
it is the courage to continue that counts.

—WINSTON CHURCHILL

Perseverance is more important than talent, intelligence and strategy. **There is great virtue in never giving up.** When life doesn't go according to plan, keep moving forward, no matter how small your steps are. **The top two habits that will decide between success and failure, between real change and staying in the same place are patience and perseverance.**

It's highly possible that before success comes, there may be some obstacles in your path. If your plans don't work out, see it as a temporary defeat, and not as a permanent failure. Come up with a new plan and try again. If the new plan doesn't work out either, change it, adapt it until it works. This is the point at which most people give up: They lack patience and persistence in working out new plans! **But watch out. Don't confuse this with persistently pursuing a plan that doesn't work!** If something doesn't work...change it! **Persistence means persistence toward achieving your goal.** When you encounter obstacles, have patience. When you experience setback, have patience. When things are not happening, have patience. Don't throw your goal away at the first sign of misfortune or opposition. Think of Thomas Edison and his 10,000 attempts to make the light bulb. Fail toward success like he did! Persistence is a state of mind. Cultivate it. If you fall down, get up, shake off the dust and keep on moving toward your goal.

The habit of persistence is built as follows:

1. Have a clear goal and the burning desire to achieve it.
2. Make a clear plan and act on it with daily action steps.
3. Be immune to all negative and discouraging influences.
4. Have a support system of one or more people who will encourage you to follow through with your actions and to pursue your goals.

10
Learn the "Edison Mentality"

I failed myself to success.

—THOMAS ALVA EDISON

*It is hard to fail, but it is worse never
to have tried to succeed.*

—THEODORE ROOSEVELT

Let's talk about failure! This subject is so important and yet so misunderstood! Paulo Coelho hits the spot when he says, **"There is only one thing that makes a dream impossible to achieve: the fear of failure."** The fear of failure is the number one dream killer, but why? Why are we so afraid of failure? Why can't we see it like Napoleon Hill, who indicated that, "Every adversity, every failure, every heartache carries with it the seed of an equal or greater benefit." Or in other words, how would our life change if we could see failure exactly like Napoleon Hill did? **Why not see it as a learning experience that is necessary for growth and which provides us with information and motivation?** What would happen if you could fully embrace the idea that in reality, failure is a sign that points toward progress?

Learn the "Edison Mentality". Edison himself said things like, "I failed myself to success" or "I have not failed. I've just found 10,000 ways that won't work." This is what enabled him to bring many of his inventions to us. The man just didn't give up!

Accept your mistakes as feedback and learn from them! Luckily, as kids we didn't have the mentality which many of us have adapted as adults—because if we did then many of us wouldn't know how to walk! How did you learn walking? By falling many times and always getting up again. Unfortunately, somewhere along the road, you picked up the idea that failure is something terrible. And as a result of this, nowadays we fail once and then stop doing things simply because it didn't work out the first time, because we got rejected, because our business venture didn't work out right away.

NOW is the time to change your mentality toward failure! Why don't you look at it in this way from now on: **Every failure is a great moment in our life, because it allows us to learn and grow from it!**

Even more and more companies nowadays are shifting to a new mentality by allowing their employees to make mistakes, because they noticed that if people are afraid to make mistakes, creativity and innovation die, and the company's progress slows down. At the end of the day, it comes down to this: **Success is the result of right decisions. Right decisions are the result of experience, and experience is the result of wrong decisions.**

Here is a story of a famous "failure" that literally failed his way to success:

- Lost job, 1832
- Defeated for legislature, 1832
- Failed in business, 1833
- Elected to legislature, 1834
- Sweetheart (Ann Rutledge) died, 1835
- Had a nervous breakdown, 1836
- Defeated for Speaker, 1838
- Defeated for nomination for Congress, 1843
- Lost re-nomination, 1848
- Rejected for Land Officer, 1849
- Defeated for Senate, 1854
- Defeated for nomination for Vice-President, 1856
- Again defeated for Senate, 1858
- Elected President, 1860

This is the story of **Abraham Lincoln**, a man we would not exactly characterize as a failure, would we?

And here are some other famous failures:

Michael Jordan: cut from his high-school basketball team.

Steven Spielberg: rejected from film school thrice.

Walt Disney: fired by the editor of a newspaper for lacking ideas and imagination.

Albert Einstein: He learned to speak at a late age and performed poorly in school.

John Grisham: first novel was rejected by 16 agents and 12 publishing houses.

J.K. Rowling: was a divorced, single mother on welfare while writing *Harry Potter*.

Stephen King: his first book "Carrie" was rejected 30 times. He threw it in the trash. His wife retrieved it from the trash and encouraged him to try again.

Oprah Winfrey: fired from her television reporting job as "not suitable for television".

The Beatles: told by a record company that they have "no future in show business".

Answer the following questions:

Have you had any failures in the last years?

What did you learn from it?

What was the positive you got out of it?

11

Get comfortable with change and chaos

Be willing to be uncomfortable. Be comfortable being uncomfortable. It may get tough, but it's a small price to pay for living a dream.

—PETER MCWILLIAMS

The way to success goes through change and chaos. For personal growth, you have to be in a constant state of feeling slightly uncomfortable. **Get into the habit of doing things that others don't want to do.** You have to choose to do what needs to be done regardless of the inconvenience! That means: to forgive instead of holding a grudge, to go the extra mile instead of saying it can't be done; to take 100 % of the responsibility for your behavior instead of blaming others.

Most of us think that to change our lives, we have to make huge changes, and then we get overwhelmed by the hugeness of the task and end up not doing anything, and get stuck with our old habits. The answer is: take baby steps! Start changing small things which don't require a big effort and those small changes will eventually lead to bigger changes.

Start changing your way to get to work, the restaurant you're having lunch at, or meet new people.

Action Steps:

1) Do something that makes you feel slightly uncomfortable every day.
2) What will you change tomorrow? Your daily routine? Exercise? Eat healthier?

12

Focus on what you want,
not on what you lack!

*It is during our darkest moments
that we must focus to see the light.*

—ARISTOTLE ONASSIS

The number one reason why people are not getting what they want is because they don't even know what they want. The number two reason is that **while they are telling themselves what they want, they are concentrating on what they don't want, and what you are concentrating on...expands! Remember to focus on what you want from now on! Where is your focus?** On the positive or the negative? On the past or the present? Do you focus on problems or solutions? This is crucial! Here is where the law of attraction goes wrong for most people and they give up! They say, "I'm attracting money," "I'm prosperous," but at the same time, they focus most of their time on the bills they have to pay, on the money that goes out, on the fact that they are not earning too much. So what happens? They attract more of the things they don't want!

You will attract more of what you focus on! Your energy will flow into the direction of your focus and your focus determines your overall perception of the world. Focus on opportunities and you will see more opportunities! Focus on success and success will come to you.

Use the following questions to change your focus:

How can I improve this situation?

What can I be thankful for?

What is great in my life right now?

What could I be happy about right now if I wanted to?

Is this still important in 10 years?

What is great about this challenge? How can I use this to learn from it?

What can I do to make things better?

13

Watch your words

But if thought corrupts language,
language can also corrupt thought.

—GEORGE ORWELL, 1984

The only thing that's keeping you from getting
what you want is the story you keep telling yourself.

—TONY ROBBINS

Watch your words! Don't underestimate them! They are very powerful! **The words that we use to describe our experiences become our experiences!** You probably encountered a situation or two in your life, when spoken words did a lot of damage. And this is true not only in talking to others, **but also talking to yourself.**

Yes, this little voice in your head—the one that just asked, "Voice, what voice?"

You are what you tell yourself the whole day! Your inner dialogue is like the repeated suggestion of a hypnotist. Are you complaining a lot? What story are you telling yourself? If you say that you are bad, weak and powerless, then that's what your world will look like! On the other hand, if you say you are healthy, feeling great, and unstoppable, you will also reflect that. Your inner dialogue has a huge impact on your self-esteem. **So be careful with how you describe yourself:** such as, "I'm lazy", "I'm a disaster", "I'll never be able to do that", or my personal favorite "I'm tired" because of course the more you tell yourself that you are tired, the more tired you will get! Watching your inner dialogue is very important! The way you communicate with yourself changes the way you think about yourself, which changes the way you feel about yourself, which changes the way you act and this ultimately, influences your results and the perception that others have of you. Keep the conversation with yourself positive, such as "I want to achieve success", "I want to be slim", "God, I am good", because your subconscious mind doesn't understand the little word "NO". It sees your words as IMAGES.

Don't think of a pink elephant! See—I bet you just imagined a pink elephant.

And—I will repeat myself—please focus on what you want. Keep in mind that your words and especially the questions you ask yourself have a huge influence on your reality. I tell my coaching clients to never tell me or themselves that they can't do something, but instead always ask **"How can it be done?"** If you ask yourself "how", your brain will search for an answer and come up with it. The good thing is that you can really change your life by changing your language, talking to yourself in a positive way, and starting to ask yourself different questions.

Why wait? Start asking yourself different questions now!

14

New habits, new life

We are what we repeatedly do.
Excellence, then, is not an act, but a habit.

—ARISTOTLE

It takes about 21 days to implement a new habit. About 2,500 years ago, the Greek philosopher Aristotle said that you change your life by changing your habits. **The coaching process is, in its essence a process of changing the client's habits over time by introducing new ways of doing things** and substituting old behaviors. The most important step in the process of changing your habits is to become aware of them! Did you hear the saying that **If you keep doing what you are doing, you will keep getting the results you are getting?** Einstein himself defined the **purest form of insanity as "doing the same things over and over, expecting a different result".**

Is this you? Don't worry and go on reading! **If you want different results in your life, then you have to start doing things differently.** You can change this and it's relatively easy if you put in some work and discipline. Develop habits that steer you toward your goals. If you do that— success in your life is guaranteed. Here are some examples of "bad" habits that might be good to get rid of: being constantly late, working late, eating junk food, procrastinating, interrupting while somebody else is talking, being a slave to your phone, etc. Our goal in this chapter is to introduce 10 new healthy daily habits into your life within the next three months. I don't want you to be overwhelmed, so why not introduce three habits each month? With time, these habits will improve your life considerably and they will substitute ineffective habits which until now have drained your energy.

Action Step:

What 10 habits are you going to introduce?

It's not necessary to introduce BIG changes. The usual habits my clients introduce are:

- Exercise three times a week.
- Focus on the positive.
- Work on your goals.
- Walk by the beach or in the woods.
- Spend more time with your family.
- Eat more vegetables.
- Meet with friends.
- Read 30 minutes a day.
- Spend 15 minutes on "alone time" a day, etc.

It helps to have a visual display! And don't forget to reward yourself for your successes!

Start RIGHT NOW by making a list of 10 daily habits you will introduce into your life from today.

15

Know yourself

Knowing yourself is the beginning of all wisdom.

—ARISTOTLE

The first step before changing your life is becoming aware of where you are and what's missing. **Please take some time to answer the following questions.**

What are your dreams in life?

_____

_____

_____

At the end of your life, what do you think you would most regret not having done for yourself?

_____

_____

_____

If time and money were not factors, what would you like to do, be or have?

_____

_____

What motivates you in life?

What limits you in life?

What have been your biggest wins in the last 12 months?

What have been your biggest frustrations in the last 12 months?

What do you do to please others?

What do you do to please yourself?

What do you pretend not to know?

What has been the best work that you have done in your life until today?

_____

_____

_____

How exactly do you know that this was your best work?

_____

_____

_____

How do you see the work you do today in comparison to what you did five years ago? What's the relationship between the work you do now and the work you did then?

_____

_____

_____

What part of your work do you enjoy the most?

_____

_____

_____

What part of your work do you enjoy the least?

_____

_____

_____

What activity or thing do you usually postpone?

_____

_____

_____

What are you really proud of?

_____

_____

How would you describe yourself?

What aspects of your behavior do you think you should improve?

At this moment in time, how would you describe your commitment level to making your life a success?

At this moment in time, how would you describe your general state of well-being, energy, and self-care?

At this moment in time, how much fun or pleasure are you experiencing in your life?

If you could put one fear behind you once and for all, what would it be?

In what area of your life, do you most want to have a true breakthrough?

_____

_____

_____

Evaluate yourself on a scale from 1–10 (10 = highest) in the following areas:

Social ———————

Work ———————

Family ———————

Interpersonal ———————

16

Know your top four values

*Efforts and courage are not enough
without purpose and direction.*

—JOHN F. KENNEDY

Let's talk about values. Not in a moral or ethical way, but
looking at what fuels you and what motivates you. Being clear
about and knowing your values is one of the most important
steps to getting to know yourself better. By knowing your values,
you will be able to attract more of what you want in your life.
If there is a big difference between the life you are living and
your values, this might create suffering and tension. Once you
find out what your values are, you will be able to understand
yourself and your actions a lot better. **When your goals are
aligned with your values, you will notice that you achieve
them much quicker and hit a lot less resistance.** Everything
changed for me around two years ago when I gained a clear
knowledge of my values. I finally knew where the tension and
stress at my work and in my life came from (not one of my
core values was being applied!) and I could understand my

reactions in various situations a lot better. So what is **really** important to you? Find out what your most important values are that bring you joy, peace and fulfillment. From the list of values, (you can download it on my webpage for free) choose 10. You may find that you can group values. **Then narrow them down to your top four values.**

Also answer the following questions:

What is very important in your life?

What gives purpose to your life?

What are you usually doing when you experience that feeling of inner peace?

What are you doing that is so much fun that you usually lose track of time?

Think of some people that you admire. Why do you admire them? What kind of qualities do you admire in them?

What activities do you enjoy the most? What kind of moments brings you joy and fulfillment?

What can't you put up with?

Visualization:

Take some time. Close your eyes and relax.

Imagine that it is your 75th birthday. You're strolling around in your house. All your friends and family are present. What would you like the most important person in your life, your best friend, and a family member say to you? Write it down.

1) The most important person in your life says....
2) Your best friend says....
3) Your (family member) says...

17

Know your strengths

*A winner is someone who recognizes his God—given talents, works
his tail off to develop them into skills, and uses
his skills to accomplish his goals.*

—LARRY BIRD

You don't have to be good at everything. Focus on your strengths.
Remember that what you focus on tends to expand. What are
you good at? Time to find out—isn't it? So let's get started:

**List your TOP FIVE Personal Qualities and Professional
Strengths below:**

(What are your unique strengths? What are you most proud
of? What do you do best?)

_____

_____

_____

List your Most Significant Personal and Professional Accomplishments:

(What are you most pleased about and proud of having accomplished?)

_____
_____
_____

List your Personal and Professional Assets:

(Who do you know? What do you know? What gifts do you have? What makes you unique and powerful?)

_____
_____
_____

Once you know your strengths, it's time to strengthen them. Practise them and concentrate on them—the ones you have and the ones you want (see Chapter 60: Fake it till you make it).

Action Step:

If you are up for it, send an email to five friends and/or colleagues and ask them what they consider your greatest strengths! This can be quite inspiring and a true self-confidence booster!

18

Honor your past achievements

The more you praise and celebrate your life,
the more there is in life to celebrate.

—OPRAH WINFREY

This is a very important chapter. It's one of my favorite exercises to boost my clients' self-confidence (and my own). Its purpose is to empower you and make you aware of what you have already achieved in your life! We are always so centered in the things that don't work so well or what we haven't achieved that we forget what we have already achieved. I'm sure that you have fantastic achievements in your life, and in this chapter, you will become aware of those past successes and use them as rocket fuel to achieve your goals and future successes! So the big question is: **What great things have you achieved in your life so far?** You put yourself through college, traveled the world, have a great career, have lots of great friends. Maybe you lived abroad for a while, all on your own. Or maybe, you have overcome a tough childhood and major personal setbacks. Maybe you raised fantastic children. Whatever challenges you've overcome or successes you have achieved, now is the time to look back and celebrate them. **Remember the chapter about focus?** In this case, it means that the more you remember and acknowledge your past successes, the more confident you'll become. And because you are concentrating on successes, you will see more opportunities for success! **Make your list! Remind yourself of your past successes! Give yourself a pat on the shoulder and say to yourself "Well done!"** The important thing is the experience of success! Get into the same state that you were in, see the success once again in your mind, feel again how it felt then!

Action Step:

1) Write down a list of the biggest successes you've achieved in your life!
2) Read them out loud and allow yourself to feel fantastic for what you have accomplished!

19

Write down your goals
and achieve them

*People with clear, written goals accomplish far more in a shorter
period of time than people without them can ever imagine.*

—BRIAN TRACY

A goal is a dream with a deadline.

—NAPOLEON HILL

The huge majority of us don't have even the slightest idea of
where to start to make our dreams come true. **Most people
overestimate what they can do in a month and under-estimate
what they can do in a year.** If you go one step at a time and
remain flexible, then over time you can achieve things that you
couldn't even imagine before. And the funny thing is: It's not
even about reaching the end goals; **it's about the person you
become in the process.** The journey is more important than
the destination—and also in goal setting! So why write down
your goals? **Because they will drive you to take action!** Having

clearly defined goals in your life is crucial to your way toward success and happiness. They are like a GPS system leading the way. But to be led, first of all you have to know where you want to go! This is so important that entire books are written on the subject of goal setting! I will make it as short as possible.

The first step to achieving your dream goals is to put them in writing. I was very skeptical about this until I started writing down my goals and then I wish I had started two decades ago. I became so much more productive and focused that I could hardly believe it. As I said before, for many years I didn't care about goal setting. To be honest, I think it made me feel uncomfortable because committing to goals and writing them down suddenly meant that I could measure what I had achieved and what I did not achieve, and I didn't have the courage to do that.

It's important to write down your goals for various reasons:

1) When you write them down, you declare to your mind, that out of the 50,000 to 60,000 thoughts you have a day, THIS ONE written down is the most important.

2) You start concentrating and focusing on the activities that bring you closer to your goal. You also start taking better decisions, while you are focused on where you want to go, always keeping in mind whether what you are doing in this moment is really the best use of your time.

3) Having a look at your written goals every day forces you to act and helps you to prioritize your actions for the day by asking yourself questions such as, "In this moment, is doing what I'm doing bringing me closer to my goals?"

Before starting the change process, you have to be clear about your goals. Then break them down into small achievable action steps and make a list of all the steps that you will take to get there. Calculate how long it will take you. Don't forget to set a deadline for each action step and goal. Don't worry if you don't reach the goal by the exact date you set; it's just a way of focusing on the goal and creating a sense of urgency. One of my favorite quotes from my coaching training is **"If you put a date on a dream, it becomes a goal."** So it's GO time for you now.

In the following exercise, I want you to write down what you want your life to look like in the next 10 years. When you write it down, I want you to **write down what you want, not what you think is possible.** So **GO BIG!** There are no limits to your imagination. The answers you write here are the direction in which your life is headed. **Create a clear vision of your goals in your mind. See yourself as already having achieved the goal: How does it feel? How does it look? How does it sound? How does it smell?**

The goals have to be yours, specific, stated positively and you have to commit to them.

Another important point: **When pursuing your goals, reward yourself for the effort put in, and not just for the results.** Self-punishment is not allowed! Keep in mind that you are much further than you were a week or a month ago.

Other useful tips that enhance your goal-setting journey:

- Put a little card with your goals written on it in your wallet and reconnect four–five times daily.
- It's very beneficial to have a to-do list. Put your action steps on it, as well as the time it takes to do the task and put the deadlines for each task.

- Balance your goals (physical, economic, social, professional, family, spiritual).

Exercise:

1) What do you want your life to look like in 10 years? There are no limits! Go big!
2) What do you need to have achieved in five years to get closer to your goal in 10 years?
3) What do you need to have achieved in a year to get closer to your goal in five years?
4) What do you need to have achieved in three months to get closer to your one-year goal?
5) What are the things that you can do NOW to reach your three-month goal?

Action Step:

Write down at least three things and TAKE ACTION!

_____

_____

_____

20
Next!

*I take rejection as someone blowing a bugle in
my ear to wake me up and get going,
rather than retreat.*

—SYLVESTER STALLONE

Another one of the biggest fears that we have is the fear of
rejection. We don't ask the girl for a dance because we fear
rejection, we don't send the CV because we fear rejection, we
don't even ask for the upgrade to business class or the best table
in the restaurant because we fear rejection! **To reach your goals
in life, you will have to learn how to handle rejection.** It's
a part of life and to overcome it, you have to become aware
that—same as failure—it's only a concept in your mind! The
most successful people are not much different from you. **They
are just better at handling rejection.** Now that's something, isn't
it? On your way to your goals, you will probably have to face
rejection many times. Just don't give up. And above all, **don't
take rejection personally.** Think about it. If you ask someone
out and he or she doesn't want to go out with you, actually

nothing has changed. He or she was not going out with you before and she is not going out with you now. Your situation is the same. **Rejection is not the problem; it's the inner dialogue you start after being rejected that is the problem:** "I knew I can't do it. I know I'm not good enough. Father was right. I will never achieve anything in life". The important thing is to go on! The most successful salesmen's goal is to hear 100 "No's" a day, because they know that if they hear 100 "No's", there will also be some "Yes's". **It's a numbers game!** The most successful "Don Juans" of my friends are the ones who dealt with the "No's" the best. They knew that if they talk to 25 girls a night, eventually there will be someone who will have a drink with them. Others gave up after hearing a couple of "No's". Just be prepared to get rejected many times on your way to success. The secret is to not give up! When somebody tells you "No, thanks" you think **"NEXT"**. Did you know that Sylvester Stallone's script for the movie "Rocky" was rejected over 70 times? Jack Canfield's and Mark Victor Hansen's "Chicken Soup for the Soul" was rejected a 130 times and that Canfield was actually laughed at when he said that he wanted to sell 1 million books. His editor told him he'd be lucky to sell 20,000. Well, the first book "Chicken Soup for the Soul" sold 8 million copies, the whole series about 500 million! Even J.K. Rowlings' "Harry Potter" was rejected 12 times!

Answer the following questions:

What are you taking away from this chapter?
How will you deal with rejection from now on?

21

Avoid energy robbers

Energy and persistence conquer all things.

—BENJAMIN FRANKLIN

The energy of the mind is the essence of life.

—ARISTOTLE

Your energy is crucial for boosting you toward your goals and happiness. There are some things in your life that drain your energy and then there are things that add energy. Don't underestimate the importance of energy and keep it up! In my coaching processes, we put a lot of emphasis on activities that bring energy and cut loose things that drain energy out of my clients' lives. When you operate on low energy, you don't feel good, you are not happy, you send out low vibes, and chances are that you will attract what you are sending! Stop doing or exposing yourself to things that drain your energy like unhealthy eating habits, alcohol, drugs, caffeine, sugar, tobacco, lack of exercise, negativity, sarcasm, unfocused goals, the news and tabloid newspapers, among others. All these things drain your energy. And beware of the "energy vampires" amongst your colleagues, friends, and even family. Why would you spend time with people that only drain you? Become very selfish on how you manage your energy:

- Eliminate all distractions.
- Finish your unfinished business.
- Work on your tolerations. (See Chapter 29)
- Say goodbye to all energy-robbing people and relationships.

Questions:

What are the energy robbers in your life?
_____
_____
_____

What will you do about it?
_____
_____
_____

22

Manage your time

*There is nothing so useless as doing efficiently
that which should not be done at all.*

—PETER F. DRUCKER

Do you work lots of overtime and still don't have time for everything you need to do? Are you one of those people that would love to have 28 hours in a day? Well, unfortunately you also have only 24 hours like everybody else on this planet. Oh and I'm sorry, I forgot: There is no such thing as time management! You can't manage time. What you can do is use your time wisely and manage your priorities. **Everyone who comes to me, including most of my friends, say, "I don't have time to_____ (fill in the blank)."** The fastest way to gain time is to watch one hour less of TV every day. That's 365 hours a year, which equals 28 hours a month! What would you do with seven extra hours a week? Another trick to gain more time is getting up earlier (see Chapter 25).

Set priorities and choose what activities to invest your time in. **Set clear rules about when you are available and when**

you are not available and don't let other people steal your time. The funny thing is, the more you value your time, the more you will have of it, because people will also value your time. If you allow people to interrupt you all the time, you're essentially showing them that your time is not very valuable, in which case, you will not be able to work effectively, no matter how many hours you work. Recent studies have found out that each five-minute interruption at work costs you 12 minutes, because your brain needs seven minutes to refocus! How many interruptions do you have per day? 10? 12? Imagine how much time you can gain back when you decrease the number of interruptions. Every three-minute interruption costs you 10 minutes. Let's say you get interrupted 12 times in one working day: that's two hours gone! In a month, that's like having an extra week! Don't let employees, friends or clients interrupt you. Set those clear rules NOW.

Another big time robber is social media and e-mail. **Setting fixed hours for your social media activity and checking emails is another means to gain a lot of time.**

I started gaining a lot of time at work when I learnt to say "NO". (See Chapter 24)

My personal number one time-saving technique is taking 30 to 60 minutes on Sundays to plan my week ahead. I put my personal and professional goals for every week in my excel sheet. **And don't forget to schedule in some free time, relaxation time,** like power naps, reading, meditation, etc. and some buffer time for emergencies too. I also take 15 minutes every day to plan my next day. In this way, I give my subconscious mind a chance to work on it already while I sleep. This works! When I start the next day I don't have to think much: I just go to work.

Some more time-saving tips:

- Make a to-do list with date and the time the task takes.
- Limit your phone calls to five minutes per call.
- Be aware of the result you want for each call that you make.
- Work against time and you'll get your work done faster (set an alarm clock and work against it).
- Write three things you want for the next day each evening and list them in order of priority.
- Create blocks of time (90-minute blocks).
- Track your time. Take a look at how you are currently using your time by tracking your daily activities.
- Do the unpleasant things first.
- Stop being busy and go for results.

Be careful with the following time robbers:

- Lack of information for completing a task.
- You do everything yourself (Is delegating an option?).
- You get distracted easily (Focus and set boundaries!).
- Your phone calls are too long (Put a five-minute limit).
- You spend a lot of time in searching for files (Get organized!)
- You keep doing things the same way and don't realize that there could be a more efficient way of doing it.
- You think you have to be reachable all the time and everywhere (Really?).

So what are you going to do next? **Will you insist on the excuse that you have no time** or will you start making time with one little thing at a time and experience the change for yourself? What are you going to do? Remember, it's all about decisions and habits!

Action Step:

Write down five things you will start doing NOW!

_____

_____

_____

_____

_____

23

Start to get organized

Organizing is what you do before you do something,
so that when you do it, it is not all mixed up.

—A.A. MILNE

For every minute spent organizing,
an hour is earned.

—ANONYMOUS

Are you too busy to get organized? You are surrounded by mountains of paper and have post-its all over your table. And you feel you are really busy, but you just can't breathe and you just can't handle your work even if you do extra time? **THEN READ CLOSELY NOW, because I'm especially talking to YOU!**

It's not that you are too busy to get organized, it's because you are not organized that you are so busy! And to make it worse: **Being busy doesn't mean that you are effective! Just because you have the messiest table in the office, doesn't mean you are the one who works hardest.**

There are studies that today's executives spend between 30% and 50% of their time searching for paperwork! Can you believe that?

So, my overwhelmed worker, go on reading and TRY OUT these little tips, as they can change your life! I have been there and I turned it around using the little tips below:

- Spend the first 15 minutes of your working day prioritizing what to do.
- Spend one hour a week organizing and filing papers.
- Spend 15 minutes a day throwing away papers and clearing away your desk.
- Spend the last 15 minutes of your working day to go through your tasks for tomorrow. What's important? What's urgent?
- Use your e-mail inbox as a to-do list. Tasks solved get archived and tasks unsolved stay in the inbox.
- If there are any e-mails and tasks that you can do in less than five minutes, always do them right away! ALWAYS!
- Don't accept any new tasks until you are in control.
- Do the job right the first time, so that it doesn't come back to haunt you and cost you more time later.

Do you remember that typical colleague who always completed his work fast, but not thoroughly and then during every step of the process you had to go back to him for more information? Instead of doing it well one time with all of the correct documentation which takes 15 minutes, he rushed it in five minutes, and later, you had to go back to him thrice, thus losing another 30 minutes. So instead of 15 minutes, he actually took 35 minutes to complete the task. Do it right the first time!

Like everything else in this book, saying "That won't work

for me" doesn't count as an excuse! Try it for at least two weeks and if it still doesn't work for you, write me an email and complain to me!

Action Step:

Which of the tips will you try first?

24
Say "NO" to them and "YES" to yourself

I don't know the key to success, but the key
to failure is trying to please everybody.

—BILL COSBY

Here is another one of these small exercises that improved my life a lot: When I stopped wanting to please others and started being myself, a lot of it came with the word "No". Every time you say "No" when you mean "No", you are actually saying "Yes" to yourself! Before learning to say "No", I often went out with my friends, although I didn't want to or went to events I didn't enjoy. The result was, I was there physically but mentally, I was in another place and honestly, I was not the best company. When I decided that a "Yes" is a "Yes" and a "No" is a "No", I felt much better. I went out less with my friends and telling them "NO" was hard at the beginning, but the result was that when I was with my friends, I was fully there.

In my work life, the impact was even bigger. When I started working in Spain, I wanted to be a good colleague and said "yes" to every favor I was asked of. Guess what happened! I ended up being totally overwhelmed at work, because I was asked a lot of favors—usually work nobody else wanted to do. It took me a while to put my foot down, but finally, I said "Enough!" From then on, my first answer to all questions for favors was "NO! Sorry. Can't do it. Very busy at the moment!" By starting to say "No" often, I improved my work life a lot and actually freed up a lot of time. But make sure you say "NO" without feeling guilty! You can explain to the person in question that it's not anything personal against them, but for your own well-being. I could still do my colleagues a favor, but only if I had enough time and decided to. Suddenly, I was in the driver's seat. If I was up for it, I would mention to the colleague in question that I'm only doing a favor and in no case do I want to end up doing the job. Selfish? Yes! But keep in mind who the most important person in your life is. That's right! YOU are the most important person in your life! You have to be well! Only if you are well yourself, can you be well toward others and from this level, you can contribute to others, but first be well yourself. You can always buy some time and say "maybe" at first, until you come to a definite decision. Life gets a lot easier if you start saying "No"!

Ask yourself the following questions:

Whose life are you living? Are you living your own life or trying to please and fulfill the expectations of others?

Who and what are you going to say NO to, starting NOW?

Action Step:

Make a list of things that you will stop doing!

25

Get up early! Sleep less!

It is well to be up before daybreak, for such habits contribute to health, wealth, and wisdom.

—ARISTOTLE

The first benefit of getting up an hour earlier is that you gain around 365 hours per year. 365! Who said "I don't have time"? When clients come to me telling me that they don't have time, the first thing I ask them is how many hours of TV are they watching. This usually provides them with the time they need. To those who stopped watching TV and still don't have enough time, I ask them to get up one hour earlier. There is a very special energy in the morning hours before sunrise. Ever since I started getting up around 5.30 or 6 o'clock, my life changed completely. I'm much more calm and relaxed and don't start the day already running around stressed. I usually go running half an hour before the sun rises, so that on my way back, I see the sun rising "out of" the Mediterranean Sea. This is absolutely mind-boggling and already puts me in a state of absolute happiness. And for those of you who don't live next to the sea, a sunrise "out of" the fields, forests, or even a big city is just as exciting. Just go watch it and let me know! Starting your day like this is very necessary for your happiness and peace of mind. Another great advantage of getting up earlier is that it reinforces self-discipline and you'll gain self-respect. Many successful leaders were and still are members of the early birds club, for example, Nelson Mandela, Mahatma Gandhi, Barrack Obama, and many more.

It's scientifically proven that six hours should be enough sleep per night, paired with a 30- to 60- minute power nap in the afternoon. Your freshness depends on the quality of your sleep, not on the quantity. You have to try and figure out for yourself how many hours of sleep you need to feel refreshed. But you should definitively give it a try. It will improve your quality of life a lot. Don't forget that getting up early is a new habit, so give it some time and don't give up after the first week if you still feel tired after getting up earlier. The habit needs at least three to four weeks to kick in. If you absolutely can't get up one hour earlier, try half an hour. And don't forget that your attitude, thoughts and beliefs about getting up an hour earlier play a big role, too. To me, it was always intriguing how it was so difficult for me to get up at 6.45ish to go to work after seven or eight hours of sleep, but before every vacation, I usually slept four hours and woke up before the alarm clock went off and I was totally refreshed and energized. **In the end, getting up or hitting the snooze button is a decision you make. It's up to you. How important is a better lifestyle and more time for you?**

26

Avoid the mass media

A democratic civilization will save itself only
if it makes the language of the image into a stimulus
for critical reflection—not an invitation for hypnosis.

—UMBERTO ECO

The news is glorified gossip.

—MOKOKOMA MOKHONOANA

You want to make fast progress, don't you? Here is one tip that will set free a lot of energy and time! How many hours do you spend in front of the "box" every day? The average American spends four to five hours a day in front of the TV, and same goes for Europeans. That's between 28 and 35 hours a week! Boom! That's a lot of time you can gain right there! Apart from gaining time, there is an even more beneficial side effect! TV is one of the biggest energy drainers, if not the number one! Do you ever feel renewed or reenergized after watching TV? **Stop watching the news, or better still turn off your television!** Why would you expose yourself to so much negativity? Don't expose yourself to too much of the garbage that is out there on TV. Substitute your habit of watching TV for a healthier habit like taking a walk, spending more time with your family or reading a good book.

I stopped watching the news many years ago when I became aware that while on the train to work, I got upset over things heard and seen on the morning news and I thought to myself, "I can't go to my stressful workplace being already stressed, simply because of what politician A said or banker B did or because there is a war in C. Just one week after stopping watching the news, I felt a lot better! Don't believe me? Just try it for yourself! **Don't watch the news for a week and see how you feel.**

I'm not telling you to become ignorant—even though here, in Spain, they say **"the ignorant is the happiest person in the village".** You can still read the newspapers. I would recommend the headlines only. You will still be up to date with the important stuff, because your family, friends, and colleagues will keep you updated. Just choose and be selective about how much garbage you expose your mind to. If you need more reasons to stop watching television, read one of the great books that are out there about how the media manipulates us and how nearly everything is fake! Control the information that you are exposed to. Make sure it adds to your life. Instead of watching trash TV, watch a documentary or a comedy. Instead of listening to the news in your car, listen to an audio—book or motivational CDs.

27

Do you "have to" or do you "choose to"?

It's choice—not chance—that determines your destiny.

—JEAN NIDETCH

Do you have many things in your life that you "should" or "have to" do, but never do? How many "shoulds" do you have in your life? Should you exercise more, go to the gym more, stop smoking, eat healthier, and spend more time with your family?

Those "shoulds" don't help you to get anywhere; they only imply that you are not good enough and just drain your energy, because they come with a bad conscience and self-torture. "Why am I not going to the gym? I'm so bad! I will never lose weight" and so on and so forth. **Make a list of all your "shoulds" and then forget it!** What? Forget it? Yes! I'm not kidding, forget it! If you have had a goal since last year and haven't done anything about it, then you are better off forgetting about it. If your goal is going to the gym and you didn't go for a year, let it go. With the goal, you also let go of the bad conscience and the self-punishment for not accomplishing it. Throw out all your "shoulds" and set some new goals!

Stop doing things that you "have to" do and instead, **choose your goals** and—very important— substitute "I should" and "I have to" with "I choose to", "I decide to", "I will" and "I prefer to".

I choose to exercise more, I will eat healthier, I choose to read more. How does that feel?

It's important that you enjoy your activities—if not, don't do them. Try out this little exercise:

I have to ——— A ——— .
If I don't do ——— A ———, then ——— B ——— will happen.
And if ——— B ——— then ——— C ——— and then ——— D ——— and ——— E ——— and then ——— Z ———.
I prefer ——— A ——— to ——— Z ——— That's why I choose ——— A ———

Action Step:

Make your list of "shoulds" and let go of them or rephrase them to "I choose to" or "I decide to".

_____

_____

28
Face your fears

The fear of suffering is worse than the suffering itself.

—PAULO COELHO

You gain strength, courage, and confidence by every experience in which you really stop to look fear in the face. You must do the thing which you think you cannot do.

—ELEANOR ROOSEVELT

Don't let your fears frustrate you, limit you or paralyze you! David Joseph Schwartz puts it this way: "**Do what you fear and your fear disappears**" and Mark Twain already knew over a hundred years ago that "**20 years from now you will be more disappointed with the things you didn't do than with the ones that you did do.**" Or as one of my favorite sayings goes: "Never regret the things you did; only those you never tried!" **So face these fears!** Ninety per cent of them are pure imagination anyway. Illusions! Incredible stories of drama and disaster that will probably never happen and are made up by your mind—"the world's greatest director of soap operas", as

T. Harv Eker says—to keep you in your comfort zone. The only problem is that great things like development, growth and success happen outside of the comfort zone.

Fear is a survival mechanism of your mind. Your mind wants to keep you safe and anything that your mind doesn't know, scares it. I had many fears in my life and still do, but I learned to overcome them and behind my fears, great opportunities waited for me. So I made it a habit to use my fear as a springboard. Just ask yourself, **"What's the worst thing that can happen to me if I do this?"** Then evaluate if the risk is worth taking or not.

Be careful! There is also a price for not taking a risk or stepping out of your comfort zone. Ask yourself, **"What price am I paying for staying the same or not doing this?"** Is it an even higher one than the price of taking the risk? This also includes intangible things like inner peace, happiness, health, etc. **Change your relationship with fear. Let it warn you and consult you, but don't let it paralyze you!** For example, I used to be totally paralyzed by fear, and stayed stuck in my job for five years because of fear of change or of the unknown. Nowadays, when I'm invaded by fears and doubts, I think to myself, "Hmm, if there are so many doubts and fears I must be on a good track. I better take action."

Try new things and attempt the seemingly impossible! Ironically, it's the things that you most fear that will be the most positive for your development and growth once you overcome them. Do the things you fear: make that call you don't want to make, send that email you don't want to send, ask that person you're afraid to ask and see what happens. When you notice fear, have a look at it, observe it, analyze it, but don't believe it. Instead ask, **"Fear, my old friend! What are you doing here**

again? Do you want to warn me or do you want to paralyze me? What's your game?"

What are you afraid of? Failure? Success? Making mistakes? Taking the wrong decisions? Do as Susan Jeffers says: "Feel the fear and do it anyway." If you want to reach new territories, you have to take some risks and continuously do things that you are afraid of. Mistakes don't matter as long as you learn from them and don't make the same mistakes over and over again. The same goes for decisions—by the way not taking a decision or procrastinating is also a decision.

Answer the following questions in your workbook or journal:

1) What is stopping you from living the life you want to live?
2) What excuses are you making for justifying staying where you are?
3) What's the worst thing that can happen if you do what you are afraid of doing?

29
Eliminate everything that annoys you

Great things are done by a series
of small things brought together.

—VINCENT VAN GOGH

It isn't the mountains ahead that wear you out.
It's the grain of sand in your shoe.

—ROBERT W. SERVICE

This is usually one of the first exercises I do with my coaching clients. **Everything that annoys you drains your energy.** In coaching, we call it tolerations. For example, a missing button on your favorite shirt, the dirty shower curtain, a kitchen cupboard that doesn't close, your boss micromanaging you, money owed to you, a disorganized guest room, broken tools, a messy and disorganized desk, clothes that don't fit any more, etc. are tolerations. For as long as you don't fix them, they keep draining your energy. As soon as you eliminate them, you will have more energy to concentrate on the things that move you forward.

So your exercise will be to make a list of all the things that annoy you: **in your private life, your job, your house, your friends, yourself, etc.**

Don't get scared if you write down 50 to 100 things. It's normal. Once you write them all down, group them. Which ones are easy to handle? Which ones can YOU handle? For now, leave the ones that don't depend on you. Have a look at them after a couple of weeks. The funny thing I've seen with my clients is that some of the tolerations that don't depend on you disappear on their own once you take care of the ones that you can handle.

For example, my client Martina had huge problems with a colleague at work. He really drained her energy. She worked on the tolerations she could handle and the list got emptier. Three months later, her colleague suddenly changed jobs and left the company! Now was that just a coincidence or was it a consequence of her working on her tolerations? I'll leave the choice to you. Fact is that she is a lot happier at work now! Try it out for yourself and keep me posted!

Action Step:

Make a list of all the things that annoy you—in your private life, your job, your house, your friends, yourself, etc.

Start working on it as described above!

30

Clean out your cupboard

Bottom line is, if you do not use it or need it,
it's clutter, and it needs to go.

—CHARISSE WARD

Do you want something new to come into your life? Do you
ever notice that as soon as you get rid of some stuff and create
space, the universe doesn't take long to fill this space again? It's
all about energy. If you have too much stuff that you don't use in
your house, it drains your energy! Coaching is about improving
your whole environment and that includes uncluttering. Start
with your cupboard. Here are some tips:

- If you haven't worn it for a year, you probably won't
  wear it any more.
- When you think "This will be useful one day" or "This
  reminds me of good times"—out it goes.

When I unclutter, I usually give stuff away for free. It just makes
me feel better and somehow, I think life/God/the universe will
reward me for it. Once you are done with the cupboard, take

on the whole bedroom. Later, move on to the living room, clean out your garage and end up cleaning up your entire home and also the office. Get rid of everything that you don't use any more: clothes, journals, books, CDs, furniture, and so on. One of my clients uncluttered his whole apartment in one weekend. He felt so much better and lighter, and got an energy boost that helped him to finish a whole bunch of his short-term goals. He never looked back. **When will you start uncluttering?**

Action Step:

Schedule a weekend and get rid of everything you don't need any more!

SCHEDULE THE WEEKEND NOW!

31

Uncluttering and tolerations go hand in hand: A real-life example

Clutter is nothing more than postponed decisions.

—BARBARA HEMPHILL

Uncluttering and tolerations go hand in hand. I have here a real-life example of my client Lawrence, who describes what happened during the process:

> *When I went through the process of uncluttering my life, it was like I was creating a new sense of freedom for myself. Before I understood what cluttering is, I had been going through life picking up so many bad habits and discouraging thoughts along the way... They weren't the type of habits like a vice, for example, smoking or drinking. They were more like small tolerations that were seemingly insignificant to begin with, but as I gained more and more of them in my life and just accepted them as something I couldn't change, they grew heavier until I was very weighed down. These tolerations made me feel like I was moving like a sloth. Things like procrastination, lack of*

sleep, not gaining fulfillment from my work, getting used to take-out food too often, beating myself up for not achieving more success... Somewhere along the way, I lost sight of my goals in life and I just allowed these tolerations to clutter things up to the point that I felt stuck.

When my coach Marc introduced the idea of uncluttering to me, it was truly a revelation. I understood what it meant immediately, but I just didn't know why I was this way or how to fix it and climb out of the hole. With the tools that Marc helped to equip me with, I can now recognize my tolerations and work on unloading them. I've identified the ones that I could fix quickly and have gotten rid of them: fixing the window sill that wouldn't open, hanging up the paintings that I left in storage when I moved, replacing my old mattress that was not so comfortable. I also recognize the tolerations that will take more time to resolve, and I work on them all the time, like challenging myself more at work and getting gratification from that productivity. I've written down all of them to keep track of and to hold myself accountable, and I write down new tolerations as I identify them along the way.

Uncluttering the tolerations in my life that were jumbled together in my mind and slowing me down, has made me feel like I am 10 times lighter now. I have more energy, more spirit, and more enthusiasm. And as I uncluttered the tolerations, I found that my physical surroundings became unclutttered as well. My apartment is cleaner and more open, so I feel like I'm in a clutter-free environment at home.

32

The most important hour...

*Write it on your heart that every day
is the best day in the year.*

—RALPH WALDO EMERSON

The most important hour of your day is composed of the 30 minutes after you wake up and the 30 minutes before you fall asleep. This is when your subconscious is very receptive, so it's of much importance what you do in this time. The way you start your day will have a huge impact on how the rest of your day develops. I'm sure you have had days which have started off on the wrong foot and from then on, it got worse and worse—or just the opposite, where you woke up with that feeling that everything will go your way and then it did. That's why it's very important to begin your day well. Most of us simply get into a rush from minute one after waking up and that's how our days unfold. No wonder most people run around stressed nowadays. What would getting up half an hour or an hour earlier every morning do for you? What if instead of hurrying and swallowing down your breakfast or even having it on the way to work, you get up and take half an hour for yourself? Maybe you even create a little morning ritual with a 10- or 15-minute meditation. Do you see what this could do for your life if you made it a habit? Here are some activities for the morning ritual. Give it a shot!

- Think positive: Today is going to be a great day!
- Remember for five minutes what you are grateful for.
- 15 minutes of quiet time.
- Imagine the day that is about to start going very well.
- Watch a sunrise.
- Go running or take a walk.
- Write in your journal.

The last half an hour of your day has the same importance. The things you do in the last half an hour before sleeping will remain in your subconscious during your sleep. So then it's time to do the following:

- Write into your journal again.
- Now is the time to reflect on your day. What did you do great? What could you have done even better?
- Plan your day ahead. What are the most important things you want to get done tomorrow?
- Make a to-do list for the next day.
- Visualize your ideal day.
- Read some inspirational blogs, articles or chapters of a book.
- Listen to music that inspires you.

I highly recommend that you NOT WATCH THE NEWS or MOVIES that agitate you before you are about to go to sleep. This is because when you are falling asleep, you are highly receptive to suggestions. That's why it's a lot more beneficial to listen to or watch positive material.

The planning ahead of your day and the list of things to do can bring you immense advantages and time saving. The things you have to do will already be in your subconscious plus you will get to work very focused the next day if you already know what your priorities are.

Questions:

How will your mornings and evenings look from now on?

Will you get up 30 minutes earlier and develop a little ritual?

What will your last activities be before you go to sleep?

33

Find your purpose
and do what you love

*The purpose of life is not to be happy. It is to be useful,
to be honorable, to be compassionate, to have it make
some difference that you have lived and lived well.*

—RALPH WALDO EMERSON

*The two most important days in your life are the
day you are born and the day you find out why.*

—MARK TWAIN

One of the most important things along your life's journey is the
discovery of your purpose. So what exactly does that mean? It
means doing what you love to do. Your answers to the questions:
"What would you do if success was guaranteed?" or **"What
would you do if you had 10 million dollars, seven houses
and have traveled to all of your favorite destinations?"** will
lead you to your purpose. You spend more time at your job
than with your loved ones, so you better enjoy what you are

doing! The 2013 Gallup "The state of the American Workplace report" states that up to 70% of people are not happy at their work! Almost 50% are not engaged, not inspired, and just kind of present and around 20% have resigned internally and are actively disengaged! I was part of the 50% for five years and it was horrible. The worst thing was that I didn't even notice it! We all have great ideas or dreams about what we could be, have, and do. What happened to your dreams? This is where the value exercise from Chapter 16 comes into the picture. The ideal picture is to build your goals around those values and have a job which allows you to live according to your values. You don't have to rush into something new, but you can start doing more of the things you love. It sounds like jargon, but when you have found your purpose, things will start to fall into place. You will start to attract people, opportunities and resources naturally and incredible things will start to happen! Nothing attracts success more than somebody who is doing what they love to do!

My friend Yvonne followed her hunch, dropped out of Law School, and started selling shoes at a big department store. She loves to help people and she loves shoes, so for her the choice was obvious. She went with her gut even though people made fun of her. She was even called the "female Al Bundy". Not a great compliment. But she didn't care about the jokes and went on to become the number one Sales Woman in the department store, selling hundreds of thousands of dollars' worth of shoes each year, taking home the Employee of the Year awards one year after another and earning a decent salary. In fact, she does so well that the VIP clients only want to be served by her. She enjoys every minute of her work.

If you feel like you are driving without a roadmap or a

GPS and don't really know where to go or if you never quite know what you are doing here and why, and you feel kind of lost and empty, then that's a sign that you have not found your purpose. But don't worry, that can be fixed in no time. You can find clues to your purpose by examining your values, skills, passions and ambitions, and by taking a look at what you are good at. Here are some more questions that should help you. Have the courage to answer them and write them down. Nobody else but you can see the answers. **(Don't skip them, like I did for 15 years! When I finally answered them, everything changed!)**

Answer yourself the following questions:

Who am I? Why am I here? Why do I exist?

What do I really want to do with my life?

When do I feel fully alive?

What were the highlights of my life?

What am I doing when time flies by? What inspires me?

What are my greatest strengths?

What would I do if success was guaranteed?

What would I do if I had 10 million dollars, seven houses, and had traveled all around the world?

Action Step:

Watch the video "What if money was no object?" (3:04) on YouTube.

34

Take a walk every day

An early-morning walk is a blessing for the whole day.

—HENRY DAVID THOREAU

Whenever possible, go out and spend time with nature. Take a walk and connect with it. Watch a sunset or a sunrise. If you are going for a run or a walk in the mornings, you'll surely say that Henry David Thoreau is right!

Our rhythm of life has become so fast and so stressful that taking some time out and walking through the woods can bring you down to earth and provide you with deep relaxation. Listen to the silence around you and enjoy it. Taking a walk is a great way to reenergize your body and your mind. **A new Stanford study that just came out concludes that walking improves your creative thinking.** When a friend 's wife had a hard time at work and was on the edge of burning out, she started taking long walks for an hour and a half each day. That helped her to disconnect from her stressful workday, forget her anger of the day, and talk about and analyze her emotions. Due to this activity, she also fell asleep easier and had a better and more refreshing sleep at night. After only a week, she felt a lot better. Another advantage of the long walks was that she got tired, lowered her guard, and even started listening to what her husband had to say ...

When will you start walking one hour per day? Do it for 30 days and let me know how it feels!

35
What are your standards?

I teach people how to treat me by what I will allow.

—STEPHEN COVEY

Expect and demand more from yourself and from those around you. If you really want to make a change in your life, you have to raise your standards. Have a zero-tolerance policy for mediocrity, procrastination and behavior that impedes your best performance! Your standards could be, for example, to always tell the truth, to always be punctual, to really listen to people until they are finished, and so on. Hold yourself to high standards and—what is of the same or even more importance— set boundaries for those around you. Boundaries are things that people simply can't do to you like yell at you, make stupid jokes around you, or disrespect you. Communicate clearly and make it a habit to address anything that bothers you on the spot. Remember what the proverb says: "In the right tone you can say everything, in the wrong tone nothing, the art is to find the right tone." Practise saying things in a neutral tone of voice like you'd say "the sun is shining".

If somebody is overstepping your boundaries, **inform** them by saying: "I didn't like that comment" or "I don't like you talking to me in that tone." If they go on, **request** them to stop: "I ask you to stop talking to me like this." By now, most people should get it, but there are always a few that continue. If that happens—**insist**: "I insist that you stop talking to me in that way." If all three steps don't help, **leave!** Walk away neutrally stating, "I can't have this conversation, while you are _____. Let's talk later."

Action Steps:

Write down the following things:

Things you will no longer accept in your life.

All the behaviors you will no longer tolerate from others.

All the things you want to become.

36

Adapt an attitude of gratitude

*Be thankful for what you have; you'll
end up having more. If you concentrate on what
you don't have, you will never, ever have enough.*

—OPRAH WINFREY

Listen to Oprah! Be grateful for what you have every day and you will attract more things to be grateful for. Gratitude recharges you with energy and boosts your self-worth. It's directly linked to physical and mental well-being. The "attitude of gratitude" leads you directly to happiness and is the best antidote to anger, envy and resentment! Let it become part of your nature. **Be grateful for what you have, for all the small things around you, and even for the things you don't have yet!**

Don't say: **"I'll be grateful when..."** like I did for many years. Take the shortcut: Be grateful NOW—no matter what—and make gratitude a daily habit. Start the day by saying "thank you" for what you have (instead of complaining about what you don't have). This will have an immediate effect on your life. Focus on the good things that you can find every day. The following exercises are part of each of my coaching processes. Do them and observe what happens.

Action Steps:

1) Make a list of everything you have in your life that you are grateful for. Write down everything you can think of. (This should be a long list)
2) For 21 days, every day, write three to five things that you are grateful for that day in your journal. Before going to sleep relive the moments. Relive the happiness.

37

The magic of visualization

The best way to predict the future is to create it.

—PETER DRUCKER

Visualization is a fundamental resource in building experiences. The subconscious part of your brain cannot distinguish between a well-done visualization and reality. This means that if you visualize your goals with a lot of emotion and in great detail, your subconscious mind will be convinced that it's really happening. You will then be provided with motivation, opportunities and ideas that will help you to transform your life into that desired state. What am I saying? Can you practise sports by pure visualization?

Well, actually you can! There are various studies that confirm the power of visualization.

As early as in the '80s, Tony Robbins worked with the U.S. Army and used visualization techniques to dramatically increase pistol shooting performance. There have also been other studies done to improve free throw shooting percentages of basketball players using the same techniques. The results were amazing!

If you look closely at athletes, they all visualize their races and matches. Look at how skiers, formula 1 drivers, golfers, tennis players, and even soccer players visualize in—game situations, days and hours before the actual match. Jack Nicklaus, Wayne Gretzky and Greg Louganis—to name a few—are known to have achieved their goals with visualization. In coaching, we use visualization techniques with goals. See yourself as already having achieved the goal. See it through your own eyes and put all your senses in it: smell it, hear it, feel it, taste it. The more emotions you put into it, the more of an impact it will have. If you do this for 15 minutes every day over time, you will see enormous results. Make time for you daily visualization either in your morning ritual or in the evening before going to bed. It can be helpful to make a collage of images that represent your goal on a A3 sheet of cardboard and put it up in your bedroom or somewhere where you can see it. Buy some journals and cut out the photos that represent your goals. You could also create a screensaver of various photos on your computer or desktop. If your goal is wealth, put a photo of you dream house, a photo of dollar bills or whatever wealth means to you. If you search for "vision board" on Google, you will surely find lots of examples. Look at your collage every day, five minutes after getting up and five minutes before going to bed and imagine yourself vividly with your goal already accomplished.

38
What if?

Our expectancies not only affect how we see reality but also affect the reality itself.

—DR EDWARD E. JONES

Always expect the best! Life doesn't always give you what you want, but it sure gives you what you expect! Do you expect success? Or do you spend most of your time worrying about failure? Our expectations about ourselves and others come from our subconscious beliefs and they have an enormous impact on our achievements. Your expectations influence your attitude and your attitude has a lot to do with your success.

Your expectations also affect your willingness to take action and all your interactions with others. Many of us know all this and yet most of us expect negative outcomes when asking one of the favorite questions of the mind—**"What if?"** By asking this question, **we are often focused on what doesn't work:** "What if it doesn't work out?" "What if she doesn't go out with me?" "What if I don't get the job?" "What if I don't get the raise?"

"What if I lose my job?" However neither does that feel

good, nor is it good to focus on what we fear. **Why not turn this around and ask yourself for every limiting or negative thought, "What if the opposite is true?"** "What if it worked out great?" "What if she says yes?" "What if I get a raise?" "What if I become a millionaire with this idea?" "What if I found resources?" "What if I can make it happen?" "What if now is the time?" "What if this little book helps me change my life for real?"

The single adjustment in how you ask a question transforms you, your energy, and the answer you get. It changes your thinking and your **inner dialogue**. Suddenly, you start asking **what if up** questions in your head, rather than **what if down** questions. The benefits of shifting your thinking will be:

- Less stress, fear and anxiety.
- You will feel more peaceful.
- Your energy level will go up.
- It allows you to be the inventor of your own experience.

Try it out! How did you feel just now reading it? Write a list of all your fears and negative "What ifs" and then turn it around.

39
Let go of the past

We must be willing to let go of the life we've planned,
so as to have the life that is waiting for us.

—JOSEPH CAMPBELL

When I let go of what I am, I become what I might be.
When I let go of what I have, I receive what I need.

—TAO TE CHING

Every moment you spend in your past is a moment you steal from your present and the future. Stop reliving your drama. Don't hang onto it. **LET GO OF IT!** Only if you have the courage to let go of the old, can you be open to new things entering your life. Don't waste your time thinking of things that could or should have happened or that didn't work out as you had wanted in the past. It doesn't make sense! You can't change it! Remember **to focus on what you want, not what you don't want.** If you focus on situations that didn't work out in the past, you might attract more of these situations. **Learn from your past experiences and move on.** That's all you have to do from now on. Easy, isn't it? Concentrate on what you want to do well in the future and not what went wrong in the past. You need to let go of the past so that you are free and new things can come into your life! Let go of old baggage, finish unfinished business and get closure with people. Deepak Chopra is right when he says, **"I use memories, but I will not allow memories to use me."** Complete the past so that you can be free to enjoy the present.

From now on, adopt the mindset that you will always finish your business. Don't leave anything incomplete in your relationships, work and all other areas. Keep moving forward.

Action Step:

What is incomplete in your life? Make a list and work on it!

40

Celebrate your wins

Celebrate what you want to see more of.

—THOMAS PETERS

On your way forward to changing your life and reaching your goals it's also important to be aware of your progress! Stop every now and then and celebrate your wins! **Celebrate that you are better than you were last week! Don't let your small victories go unnoticed.** During the work with my clients, one of their consistent tasks is to celebrate their small wins. Every action step completed is worth celebrating. **For every exercise in this book that you complete, reward yourself:** buy yourself something you always wanted, go to the movies, do whatever feels good for you. **If you learnt new habits and see great improvement, go on a short trip. You earned it. What will you reward yourself with for your progress so far?** Will you have a spa day or a nice dinner? Will you go for a walk?

1. _____
2. _____
3. _____
4. _____
5. _____

41

Be happy NOW

Happiness is the meaning and purpose of life.

—ARISTOTLE

Happiness is a journey, not a destination! Happiness is also a choice! It is an inner state, not an external state. Happiness is a habit, a state of mind. Happiness is so many things!

But the decisive and most important thing is: **What is happiness to YOU?** You can be happy right now! You don't believe me? Okay. Close your eyes for a moment. Think of a situation that made you really, really happy. Relive this situation in your mind. Feel it, smell it, hear it! Remember the excitement and joy! And? How did it feel? Did it work? How are you feeling now? Happiness doesn't depend on your car, your house or anything in the outside world. You can be happy right here, right now! Don't miss out on the small pleasures of life, while you go after the big ones. Enjoy the beauty around you! Enjoy the small things! Don't postpone life until you win the lottery or retire. Do the fun things now with what you have. Live each day fully as if it were your last! Start by being happy now. Smile as much as you can—even if you are not in the mood, because by smiling you're sending positive signals to your brain. Fun and humor are essential for a good, long life, job satisfaction, personal fulfillment, personal relationships and life balance. So laugh lots and have lots of fun! Which of these reasons do YOU have right now for being happy?

- You have a great job.
- You love your work.
- You have great kids.
- You have a great partner.
- You have great parents.
- You are free.
- ...

Questions

What is happiness to you? (Be specific.)

How many smiles have you gifted last week?

How many smiles have you received?

Action Steps:

Remember the moments that made you the happiest in your life. Write down at least five moments that made you feel exceptionally great:

1. _____

2. _____

3. _____

4. _____

5. _____

Re-live these moments with all their emotions and happiness. How does it feel?

42

Multitasking is a lie

Most of the time multitasking is an illusion.
You think you are multitasking, but in reality you're
actually wasting time switching from one task to another.

—BOSCO TJAN

DO one thing at a time! The newest studies show that multitasking is actually less productive than doing one thing at a time with a concentrated effort. Some studies even imply that it makes you slower and—careful now—dumber!

Even if you think you are multitasking, you are actually doing one thing at a time, aren't you? You might have five tasks on your hands, but I'm sure you don't do all five things at the same time. You are writing an e-mail. You stop writing it and take a phone call. You hang up and continue writing the e-mail. A colleague comes to you with a question. You stop writing your e-mail and answer the question, and so on. So forget about multitasking. Focus on doing one thing at a time and do it with concentration.

43

Simplify your life

Life is really simple, but we insist on making it complicated.

—CONFUCIUS

*The key is not to prioritize what's on your schedule,
but to schedule your priorities.*

—STEPHEN COVEY

If you started applying some of the things that you have learnt until now in this book, your life should already be a little simpler. Did you unclutter? Clean out your cupboard? Get rid of some toleration? Did you get rid of some of the people who drag you down? It was Stephen Covey who said that "most of us spend too much time on what is urgent and not enough time on what is important". Do you know your priorities or are you just floating around handling whatever comes up, extinguishing fire all the time? Maybe it's time to make some time for the really important stuff in your life. **A huge step toward simplifying your life is to concentrate on the important, on the activities that make sense for you and find a way to eliminate or downsize the**

other activities. This can be done by automating, delegating, eliminating or hiring help. **If you want to do everything, in the end you'll get nothing done.** Is your schedule too busy? Do you have too many commitments? Simplifying is about downsizing your life and learning to live with less. **What can you downsize?** Do you own too many clothes and items? Are you spending too much time cooking? Why not get help or just prepare simpler meals? Which family member can support you? Can you simplify your financial life by online banking? Why not pay everything in cash and buy only things you really need? What about your online life? Do you spend too much time on social media or instant messaging? Then, it might be time to get a little bit more disciplined. Set fixed time for when you will be online and stick to them. Put a timer if necessary. Unclutter the desktop on your PC and your e-mail inbox. My client Marc did this and virtual uncluttering had the same effect on him as physical uncluttering. He let go of a big weight that he was carrying around and hence, got a lot more energy. Check your e-mails only at certain times during the day and turn off the tone of e-mail and text delivery so that you are not distracted all the time. Now is also a good time to unsubscribe from journals that are just piling up and that you never read, and to ask yourself if you really need to read three different newspapers every day. Are you commuting to work? Maybe you can ask your boss if you can work from home once or twice a week. Are you working too many hours? See if the chapters in this book on time management and getting organized can help you to reduce your working time and find more time to do the things you love. And do yourself a favor: Don't bring your work home—not physically and not even mentally. If you didn't get it done at work, examine your working habits and change them if possible. This is extremely important. **Stop thinking about work when you are home. Worrying about something that can't be changed at the moment is wasted energy.** Think about what you can do about it tomorrow at work and forget about it for now.

Questions:

- Where do you see the excess in your life?
- Do you have too many things you don't need or use?
- Is your schedule always booked?
- Do you have time in your schedule for yourself and the things you enjoy doing?
- What are the most important tasks in your day-to-day life (home and/or work)?
- Which of these tasks can be easily delegated, automated or eliminated?

44

Smile more!

Sometimes your joy is the source of your smile, but sometimes your smile can be the source of your joy.

—THÍCH NHÂT HANH

Smile! Even if you don't feel like it! Smiling improves the quality of your life, health and relationships. If you don't do it already, start to smile *consciously* today. Although I can't confirm the study cited in many self-help books and blogs that 4- to 6-year-olds laugh 300–400 times a day and adults only 15, it might well be true. Just take our personal experiences with kids and honestly it fits very well with the results of the study. **What is confirmed is that laughing and smiling is extremely good for your health. Science has demonstrated that laughing or smiling a lot daily improves your mental state and your creativity. So laugh more.** Make it a point to watch at least an hour of comedy or fun stuff a day and laugh until tears roll down your cheeks. You'll feel a lot better and full of energy once you start this habit. Try it out.

A study by Tara Kraft and Sarah Pressman at the University

of Kansas demonstrated that smiling can alter your stress response in difficult situations. The study showed that it can slow your heart rate down and decrease stress levels—even if you are not feeling happy. Smiling sends a signal to your brain that things are all right. See also Chapter 60 (Fake it till you make it) and Chapter 61 (Change your posture). Just try it next time you feel stressed or overwhelmed, and let me know if it works. If you think you have no reason at all to smile, hold a pen or a chopstick with your teeth. It simulates a smile and might produce the same effect. If you need even more incentives for smiling, search for the study by Wayne University on smiling which has found a link between smiling and longevity. When you smile, your entire body sends out the message "Life is great" to the world. Studies show that smiling people are perceived as more confident and more likely to be trusted. People just feel good around them. Further benefits of smiling are that it:

- Releases serotonin (makes us feel good);
- Releases endorphins (lowers pain);
- Lowers blood pressure;
- Increases clarity;
- Boosts the functioning of your immune system;
- Provides a more positive outlook on life (Try being a pessimist while you smile…).

Exercise:

For the next seven days, stand in front of a mirror and smile to yourself for one minute. Do this at least three times a day and observe how you feel.

45

Start power napping

When you can't figure out what to do, it's time for a nap.

—MASON COOLEY

It is one of my absolute favorites. And at the same time, it's scientifically proven that a power nap at midday re-energizes, refreshes and increases productivity. For me, it was an absolute eye-opener. During my most stressful period at work—when I was close to burning out, as the stress, and client threats and complaints were getting unbearable (sometimes, I thought we were doing emergency surgery, yet we were just producing books), I started taking a power nap and the change was extraordinary. I was far less stressed and a lot calmer while hearing out complaints and finding solutions. For a while, I slept for 25 to 30 minutes on a bench in a park close by and later, I just put two chairs together in the office and slept there. It felt as if my working day suddenly had two halves and midday was halftime. I started the "second half" always fresh and I also performed a lot more productively because the typical tiredness after lunch between 2 and 5 p.m. was gone. **Are you going to try power napping? When will you start?**

46

Read for half an hour each day

*The man who doesn't read has no advantage
over the man that can't read.*

—MARK TWAIN

If you read for half an hour a day, that's three and a half hours
a week and 182 hours a year! That's a lot of knowledge at your
disposal. One of my first written goals during my coaching
training was "to read more". That was at a time when I hadn't
read a book for years. Now I'm devouring an average of two
books a week. I read more in the last six months than I did in
the whole 15 years before—including my International Business
studies. So always **have a book with you.** If you substitute the
habit of watching TV or the news by reading a good book just
before going to bed, you will derive the additional benefit of
peace of mind. Another positive side effect is that you increase
your creativity. So what are you waiting for? Make a list of
the six books that you will read in the next three months!
If you don't know what to read, check out my webpage for
recommendations. **But make that list NOW!**

47

Start saving

*Personally, I tend to worry about what
I save, not what I spend.*

—PAUL CLITHEROE

This one is taught by all the wealth gurus. I read it for the first time many years ago while reading Talane Miedaner's book "Coach yourself to success". This single advice changed really everything for me and was the basis for leaving my job and following my dream many years later. Once you have saved enough living expenses for nine months to one year, things start changing. This is a huge advantage. For example, you stop depending of your boss's mood. You can stand up for yourself and say: "If you have problems with my work, just tell me so." If at your current job people are not respecting your boundaries or even harassing you, in the worst case you can even quit your job and find another one. Or take a sabbatical. Furthermore, you are not desperate when you're going to job interviews because you don't need the new job that badly. As a coach, for me it was and still is important to always have a reserve, so that I have the freedom to work only with my ideal clients and can afford to say "No" to clients that aren't a fit (which a coach should do anyway, because coaching only works if the "chemistry" is right). Working out of a need for money surely wouldn't bring as good results. Having a reserve of nine, 12, or even 18 months' salaries (the more the better!) saved up just takes a lot of stress off and makes you feel a lot more secure and gives you peace of mind. To start saving, you have to spend less or earn more. Most of the time, it's easier to cut down your spending and take a look at where your money is going. The best way is to automatically deduct the sum from your account at the beginning of the month and put it into a savings account.

Questions:

Will you give it a shot?

When will you start saving?

48

Forgive everybody
who has wronged you
(...and most of all yourself)

*The weak can never forgive. Forgiveness is the
attribute of the strong.*

—MAHATMA GANDHI

*People can be more forgiving than you can imagine.
But you have to forgive yourself. Let go of what's
bitter and move on.*

—BILL COSBY

Forgiveness is crucial along your way toward success, fulfillment
and happiness. Personally, I needed a long, long time to learn
this. Why forgive someone if the person did me wrong and it's
only their fault? **The short answer: It's a selfish act!** You're doing
it for yourself, not for the other person. This is not about being
right or wrong. This is about you being well and not losing a
lot of energy. Anger and resentment and—even worse—reliving

hate over and over again are huge energy drainers. Who has sleepless nights? Who is full of anger and doesn't enjoy the present moment? You or the person you're not forgiving? Do yourself a favor and let go!

When a journalist asked the Dalai Lama whether he is angry at the Chinese for occupying his country, he answered: "Not at all. I send them love and forgiveness. It's of no benefit at all to be angry at them. It will not change them, but I could get an ulcer from my anger and that would actually benefit THEM." Adapt the attitude of the Dalai Lama toward the people who have done you wrong and see what happens. Let go, forgive the people that hurt you, forget them and move on. But be careful. **If you say, "I forgive them, but I don't forget", you are not forgiving.** This doesn't mean you can't put limits on others' behavior or call them out on the spot. But afterwards understand the consequences and let go. Call up people that you have wronged or hurt, and apologize, and if that's too uncomfortable, write them a letter. **Above all: forgive yourself! When you learn to forgive yourself, it will be easier to forgive others.** Just do it! The changes you will see when you manage to forgive others and above all, yourself are amazing.

Action Steps:

1. Make a list of everybody that you haven't forgiven.
2. Make a list of everything that you haven't forgiven yourself for.
3. Work on the list.

Questions:

What would your life be like if you accepted yourself just as you are, without any self-criticism?

What would your life be like if you forgave yourself and others?

49

Arrive 10 minutes early

The while we keep a man waiting,
he reflects on our shortcomings.

—FRENCH PROVERB

Punctuality is a sign of discipline and respect for others. Without it, you might come across as slightly offensive, even if you are the nicest person in the world. Of course, there are cultural differences. For example, while in Mexico and Spain people are very relaxed about punctuality, in Germany not being punctual is seen as highly unprofessional and might ruin your chances in any endeavor. Here is another great tip from Talane Miedaner's book, "Coach yourself to success", which I have made into a habit: be punctual not to be especially polite, but instead for myself. This is because when I started being punctual, I noticed that those 10 minutes made me feel a lot better and gave me a lot of peace of mind. When I arrived at a place, it wasn't in a rush and I actually had 10 minutes to compose my thoughts and get used to the environment. Instead of feeling rushed, I felt very relaxed. I also feel very comfortable, professional and polite when I arrive 10 minutes early. In fact, I now feel uncomfortable when I arrive just on time. **Try it and see for yourself if it adds to your life or not.**

50

Speak less, Listen more

When people talk, listen completely. Most people never listen.

—ERNEST HEMINGWAY

One of the most important tools of a coach and also one of the most important lessons from my coaching training is the ability and skill of "active listening" or listening profoundly.

Listening profoundly means to listen to the person in front of you while giving your full attention. It means to quiet down the little voice in your head that comes up with advice and a solution 30 seconds after the person starts speaking. **Many people are not listening to understand, but to answer.** They are just waiting for their counterpart to pause so that they can begin to speak. **If you are rehearsing what you are going to say next, you are not listening.** Don't interrupt. Listen until the person is finished. If you want to give advice, ask for permission. Most of the time, the person who is speaking will come up with the solution—if you let her or him finish. Try it! You might take your conversations and relationships to a completely new level when, people feel that they are listened to by you. Be a good listener!

51

Be the change you want to see in the world

Be the change you want to see in the world.

—MAHATMA GANDHI

Are you trying to change other people? I've got news for you: You can stop right NOW. **It's impossible!** You can't help people who don't want to get help and you just can't change other people. So stop wasting your precious energy and start concentrating on what you can do. And that is being an example! **Be the change you want to see in the world!**

Have you heard about the idea that other people are like mirrors of us? That means that things we don't like about them, are often things we have to work on ourselves and/or balance them out. When I was "stuck", I always got mad at the lack of manners in young people who didn't offer their seats to elderly people on the train. Whenever I observed this, I used to start a negative inner dialogue about "where the world is going, this can't be, young people have no manners, why should I get up, I'm 40 years old, blah blah". Until one day I stopped complaining about the young people and offered my seat. Man, that felt good! **I'm not responsible for other people's behavior. I'm only responsible for my own behavior.** So by being an example, I win twice: Once by not having this inner nagging dialogue and secondly, because I feel like I did something right and that feels so good. And maybe I even served as an example to somebody else to offer his or her seat the next time. One of the greatest insights that my clients have is when they shift from **"others have to change"** to **"what if I change, maybe then the other also changes".** You can literally see the light bulb go on over their heads. You cannot change others. The only thing you can to do is accept them as they are and be the best example and person that you can be. Are you complaining about your partner, colleagues or spouse? **Be the best colleague or spouse possible! Are you complaining about your employees? Be the best boss possible! Do you want to be loved just as you are? Start with loving other people just the way they are.**

Questions:

What do you want to change?

Why not start with yourself?

What will you do differently?

52

Stop trying and start doing

Try not. Do or do not. There is no try.

—MASTER YODA, "STAR WARS"

You can do yourself a huge favor if you stop using the word "try". Throw it out of your vocabulary! **Trying implies failure.** What would you rather have a person say to you if you put them in charge of a task: "I'll try to get it done" or "I'll get right on it"? **Do or do not!** When I was at the beginning of my coaching career, I found out quick that those of my clients who tried to do their homework, usually didn't do it. Those who tried to find more time, didn't find it. Those who tried to exercise three times a week, didn't do it. From then on, when someone said to me, "I'll try", I asked them, "Will you do it or won't you?" **There is no try!** It's as Nike says, "Just do it!" If you do it and it works…great! Well done! If you do it and it doesn't work. Ok. Let's have a look at it. What went wrong? Did you learn something from the experience? What can you change to get the result you want? Go again! **Just trying doesn't take you anywhere. I'm in line with Master Yoda: Do or do not!**

53

The power of affirmations

*Here is a most significant fact—the subconscious
mind takes any orders given it in a spirit of absolute
FAITH, and acts upon those orders, although the orders often
have to be presented over and over again, through repetition,
before they are interpreted by the subconscious mind.*

—NAPOLEON HILL, "THINK AND GROW RICH"

We already talked about the importance of positive self-talk.
One very good technique is using Affirmations. By repeating
positive statements many times a day you convince your
subconscious mind to believe them. And once your subconscious
mind is convinced, you start acting accordingly and "attract"
circumstances into your life and see opportunities everywhere.
It's important to state them positively and in the present so
that your subconscious mind can't differentiate between if it's
already true or "only" imagined. **Affirmations do have to be
personal, positively stated, specific, emotionally charged and
in the present tense.** Here are some examples:

- Money comes to me easily and effortlessly.

- Opportunities come into my life right now.
- Speaking in front of a large audience is easy for me.
- I am successful in my business.
- I am healthy and fit.

Use affirmations to attract the things you want in your life. The more you practise, the better you get. The first time you say, "Money comes to me easily and effortlessly", your inner voice will still say, "Yeah right! No way!" However after repeating it 200 times every day for a week you should have silenced your inner critical voice. Make your affirmations your permanent company. Repeat them as often as you like and have a look at what happens in your life. Nevertheless, there are some studies that claim that affirmations actually have negative effects, when your inner critic just doesn't get convinced. If you can see no benefit at all, try other techniques like subliminal tapes or ask yourself other questions such as, "Why am I so happy? Why is everything working out?"

Noah St. John has written a whole book, "Book of Afformations", on the power of asking yourself the right questions. Read it. It might be able to help you!

54
Write it down 25 times a day

It's the repetition of affirmations that lead to belief.
And once that belief becomes a deep conviction,
things begin to happen.

—MUHAMMAD ALI

The purpose of this exercise is to help you "hammer" your desires into your subconscious mind until you actually believe it's true. Remember how your subconscious mind works. To create a new belief in your belief system, you have to repeat it over and over again. Even if this exercise gets boring, go on writing! So how does it work?

1) Pick your statement.
2) Make it personal, start with "I am".
3) Make the statement positive.
4) Use present tense. For example, "I am earning X thousand Euros a year."
5) Do this exercise first thing in the morning.

It's good to get a small booklet for it. You can enhance your results by doing the exercise twice a day: in the morning and just before going to sleep.

55
Stop making excuses

*The only thing standing between you and
your goal is the bullshit story you keep telling
yourself as to why you can't achieve it.*

—JORDAN BELFORT

What happens when you start stepping out of your comfort zone?
Due to fears and doubts, your mind comes up with the greatest
excuses: It's not the right moment, I'm too young , I'm too old,
It's impossible, I can't, and my favorite one, I have no money.
Guess what people with money say: I have no time. "Yes, but
my case is different," you might say. No, it's not! Believe me.
The right moment never comes, so you might as well start here
and now or wait forever. A crisis is always an opportunity. You're
neither too young, nor too old. Do a search on the Internet.
It's full of stories of people who fulfill their dreams at an older
age or start an enterprise at a young age. No money? Or just
spending it in the wrong places by buying a new TV or video
game console instead of investing it in your training? The funny
thing is people who work with a serious financial advisor or

financial coach suddenly find money. In the same way as all of my clients who thought they didn't have time found time. "Yes, but my case is different!" Well, you can keep telling that to yourself for some more time or you get rid of the excuses once and for all and start taking action, because one thing is for sure: If you keep doing what you are doing you will keep getting what you are getting! So what is it going to be?

Questions:

What are you going to choose from now on? Excuses or focused action?

What are the excuses you are using to not change and stay in the same place?

56

Keep expectations low and then shine

Always deliver more than expected.

—LARRY PAGE

This is another biggie and probably the best time management trick I ever learnt. It changed my professional and private life in an extraordinary manner and reduced stress at work to virtually zero! Most of my stress at work came from deadlines, and I or we, as an enterprise, were always struggling, which made days when our products were shipped to the clients—which was every day in high season—horrible and very stressful. We were always just in time or sometimes maybe a couple of hours late and I had to calm down angry and sometimes hysterical clients... until I started to under promise. I figured out that over 90% of our late deliveries were just a question of a couple of hours, so I got the permission of my boss and started my own delivery schedule that only I received access to. If production gave me a delivery date of April 5th, I told the client April 10th. So, if we delivered on April 7th, instead of an angry client threatening to fine or sue us, I suddenly had extremely grateful clients who thanked me for delivering three days early. Within a short time, we reduced late deliveries from nearly 50% to virtually 0% over the next three years. As it worked out so well, I started applying it to my whole life. When my boss gave me a project that took me three days, I told her I was going to need five. If I had it completed after four days, I looked great and if I took a little longer, I was still on time—and spending without weekends at the office. If I knew I had to stay at work longer, I told my wife I'll be home at 9 p.m. Coming home at 8:30 p.m., I looked like a hero. Careful here! This worked for me. My colleagues who knew the trick always warned me that one day I could encounter an unpleasant surprise in the cupboard... Well these are things we see in movies...

57
Design your ideal day

You'll see it when you believe it!

—DR WAYNE W. DYER

This is the favorite exercise of many coaches and the starting point for many coaching processes. **Design your ideal day! What would you like your ideal life to be? What would you do if you had all the time and money in the world? Where would you live? Would you have a house or an apartment? What's your job? Who are you with? What are you doing?** It's time to dream big again. Don't limit yourself. Imagine your ideal life vividly. How does it feel?

Write it down in detail. By now, you have learnt about the power of writing things down. **Write down exactly how you would like your ideal life to be.** Have a special notebook or scrapbook for your ideal day/life creation. Many people even make a collage with photos that represent their dreams or ideals and put it up somewhere where they can see it daily. Very important: Make it FUN! It's very important to create this vision and have it in mind. So let's start:

1) No distractions. Sit down for an hour. Turn off everything. No cell phone, no radio, no TV.
2) Make it come alive! Describe everything. What time do you wake up? What kind of home do you live in? How's your health? Who is surrounding you? What's your job? Remember there are NO LIMITS!
3) Once a week, read your ideal day out with enthusiasm. Put a lot of emotion into it!

Optional:

You can also tape-record yourself reading out your ideal day with emotion and listen to it every night before going to bed.

Are you ready? Start writing out your ideal day right now!

58

Accept your emotions

Your intellect may be confused,
but your emotions will never lie to you.

—ROGER EBERT

Who is responsible for how you feel? YOU! Do you remember what we said about responsibility and choices? Do you remember that you are in control of your thoughts? Well, your emotions come from your thoughts. How?

An emotion is energy in motion, a physical reaction to a thought. If you can control your thoughts, you are also capable of controlling your emotions. Don't be scared by them. Your emotions are part of you, but they are not YOU. Accept them. Every emotion has its function. Fear protects you. Anger allows you to defend yourself, put limits on and show others what bothers you. Sadness allows you to mourn and identify a lack. Happiness allows you to feel great, and so on. It's very important to be connected to your emotions and know how to express them and not to neglect them.

Don't fool yourself and say "I'm happy" if you're not.

Instead, analyze where the emotion comes from. Don't identify yourself with the emotion. I repeat, you are not your emotions. Become an observer and watch where your emotions lead you. Observe them and watch them pass by like the clouds in a blue sky. Accept them like you accept rainy days. When you look out of the window and see that it's raining, you don't think that it will rain all the time now, do you? You accept the rain as part of the meteorological climate—that doesn't mean that it rains all the time. You can do the same thing with anger, sadness, fear and other emotions. Just because they show up at one moment in time doesn't mean that they will be there forever. **It helps to know that emotions are not bad or good. They just are.** If you want to write something to get them out of your system—do it. They will pass. Emotions are messengers that we feel in our body. Listen to them! If you are hooked to an emotion, you are hooked to the past and you are losing the present moment. What is it you really need? Stop searching outside and start searching inside of you.

MANAGING EMOTIONS

It's the skill to perceive, use, understand and manage emotions. You can use this on yourself or on others:

1) Perceive and express emotions (Permit yourself to feel it).
2) Facilitation of feelings (How can I feel a different emotion?).
3) Understanding (Why is this emotion coming up?).
4) Emotional adjustment (Now I know why I experienced/ felt that emotion...).

Once again, everything is a question of attitude—acceptance or refusal.

YOU CHOOSE!

Advantages of managing emotions:

- You recover better and faster from problems and setbacks.
- You achieve better and consistent professional performance.
- You are able to prevent those tensions from building up that destroy your relationships.
- You govern your impulses and conflicting emotions.
- You stay balanced and serene, even in critical moments.

The first step toward getting there is to **identify** your emotions and to **explore** them, which means to **permit their expression** and then **analyze** the problem/situation that provoked them. Connect and talk to the emotion: breathe, relax and relive the situation.

Questions:

Can you spot a "negative" emotion?

What symptoms do you feel and in what part of your body?

How do you feel? Be precise!

59
Do it now

*You cannot escape the responsibility of
tomorrow by evading it today.*

—ABRAHAM LINCOLN

*Only put off until tomorrow what you are
willing to die having left undone.*

—PABLO PICASSO

Listen to Dr Wayne W. Dyer when he says, "Go for it now. The future is promised to no one." That unwritten e-mail, the old friend you want to reconnect with, the time you want to spend with your family: don't put it off any more. Do yourself a favor and stop the procrastination. It only causes anxiety. And most of the time, you will find that things that you procrastinated for days causing yourself anxiety and a bad conscience are actually done in an hour or so, and afterwards, you feel so much lighter because you can forget about it.

Procrastinating is avoiding something that should be done. It's putting things off hoping that they magically get better without actually doing anything about them. But things don't get better on their own. Most of the time, the cause of procrastination is some kind of fear. Fear of rejection, fear of failure, even fear of success. Another cause is feeling overwhelmed. We procrastinate in these ways:

1) Doing nothing instead of what we are supposed to do.
2) Doing something less important than what we should be doing.
3) Doing something more important that what we are supposed to do.

As a freelancer and owner of his time, my client Marc struggled with procrastination a lot. It caused him a lot of anxiety and even cost him some sleepless nights. It was always the same pattern. He procrastinated and felt burdened and anxious. In our coaching sessions, he admitted that some of the stuff that causes this anxiety, he could actually finish in an hour! He became aware that he was paying a high price for procrastinating, and in the future, when tempted to procrastinate, he decided to ask himself: what price will I be paying for procrastinating this task? Is it worth to be burdened by and lose my sleep over a task that I could have finished in a couple of hours? So do whatever it is that you have on your mind right now. **Don't start tomorrow or next week! Start NOW!**

Questions:

What are you procrastinating?

Are you productive or are you just being busy?

What is really important right now?

60

Fake it till you make it

If you want a quality, act as if you already have it.

—WILLIAM JAMES

Act as if! Act as if you have already achieved your goal. Act as if you already have the quality of life, the lifestyle, the job that you aspire for. If you want to have more self-confidence, act as if you already have it. Speak like a self-confident person, walk like a self-confident person, have the body posture of a self-confident person (See Chapter 61). Your subconscious can't differentiate between reality and imagination. Use this to your advantage by acting "as if" you already have a strength, a character trait, and so on. In Neuro-linguistic Programming and coaching, this is called modeling. A good way to become successful is to observe and imitate people who are already successful. Use this for any character trait you want. Start acting "as if" and see what happens. Fake it till you make it!

Questions:

Which quality do you want?

How would you act if you already had that quality?

How would you speak, walk, behave, and so on?

61

Change your posture

Act the way you'd like to be and soon
you'll be the way you'd like to act.

—BOB DYLAN

This is an exercise taken from Neuro-linguistic Programming which proclaims that changing your posture also changes your mind. People I tell this to usually think that I'm joking. But before writing this off as nonsense...try it out!

When you feel sad and depressed, you usually look at the floor, keep your shoulders down and adapt the posture of a sad person, right? Now try the following just for a moment: stand upright, shoulders up, chest out and hold your head up high—you can even exaggerate it by looking up. How does it feel? If you smile, laugh and walk with your head held high, you will realize that you feel a lot better. It's impossible to feel sad walking around like that, isn't it? And there has been more research conducted on this subject. A study by Brion, Petty and Wagner in 2009 found that people who were sitting straight had higher self-confidence than people sitting slumped over! There is also an amazing TED Talk by Amy Cuddy called "Your body language shapes who you are" about the research she did together with Dana Carney at Harvard University. The study has shown that holding "power postures" for two minutes creates a 20% increase in testosterone (which boosts confidence) and a 25 % decrease in cortisol (which reduces stress). Imagine this. If you have an important presentation, reunion or competition, just take on the posture of a confident person for two minutes. Put your hands on your hips and spread your feet (think Wonder Woman) or lean back in a chair and spread your arms. Hold the posture for at least two minutes…and see what happens!

62

Ask for what you really want

Ask and you shall receive.

—MATTHEW, 7, 7

Just ask! It's far better to ask and get rejected that to not ask and go along with the thought "if I had only asked". Ask for a better table in the restaurant, ask for the upgrade at the airport and ask for the salary raise you have been waiting for. ASK! You already have the "No" for an answer, but maybe you will see some surprises. If you ask, you at least have the opportunity to get what you want. Ask your loved ones for what you want. Ask your boss, your friends. **Don't expect them to read your mind!** Think about it! Aren't many things that hurt us based on the too high expectations that we had? This happened to me mostly in my romantic relationships. I was disappointed many times because my loved one just wasn't able to read my mind. That is, until I said, "That's it" and finally started asking for what I wanted. Another example is our boss! We are putting in so much work and are waiting for this raise or promotion to come, but it doesn't come! Ask for it! What's the worst thing that could happen? You already don't have it. You already haven't gotten the raise or the promotion! If you don't ask for it, it will surely stay like this. If you ask, you will at least get an answer and know where you are at. **When you ask, keep the following things in mind:**

1) Ask with the expectation to receive.
2) Know that you can receive it.
3) Remember to keep your thoughts, feelings and inner dialogue positive.
4) Ask the person who is in charge.
5) Be specific.
6) Ask repeatedly like you did when you were a kid.

Action Steps:

1) Write a list of all of the things that you want and don't ask for.
2) Start asking. Work on it.

63

Listen to your inner voice

*The intuitive mind is a sacred gift and the
rational mind is a faithful servant.
We have created a society that honors the
servant and has forgotten the gift.*

—ALBERT EINSTEIN

Albert Einstein already knew about the great gift our intuition can become for us! Listen to your inner voice, go with your hunches. It's not easy to distinguish your intuition from the "other" little voice in your head—the one that comes from rationality and often tells you what you should do or can't do. You will need to practise a little. Start with little things. For example, which road to take to work each morning, or whether to take your sunglasses with you although it's a totally cloudy day.

I remember practising my intuition when I went to high school. There were two ways to get to school and both had a train crossing with trains coming from different directions (both train crossings were very rarely closed at the same time). I made it a game to consult with my inner voice as to which way to go—sometimes following the intuition, and sometimes going against it—just to get to stop in front of the closed train crossing.

Some weeks ago, I was driving on the German Autobahn and I had two options to get to my destination. I wanted to take one road, but I had a very strong hunch to take the other one, even though it looked very crowded. Thirty minutes later, I heard on the radio that there was a 25 km traffic jam on the other autobahn! We would have been stuck right there! I thanked my inner voice right away…!

You probably already have experienced intuition. Did it ever happen to you that you thought of a person and just a second later, the phone rings and it's that person? Or you think of somebody and a minute later, you run into them at the shopping center? The more you practise and trust in this inner voice, the stronger it gets, the more results you are going to see and the easier it will be to distinguish it from the other little rational voice in your head. It's amazing! Meditation has been proven to be a great tool to get closer to your intuition. Just sit still for five or 10 minutes and listen to what's coming up. **Once you've learned to listen to your intuition, act on it immediately! It can be a hunch to write an e-mail, or to talk to somebody. If it comes in the form of an idea, act on the idea.**

64
Write in your journal

Everyone thinks of changing the world,
but no one thinks of changing himself.

—LEO TOLSTOY

I wouldn't miss this exercise for the world! An important exercise that I recommend to all of my clients: have a journal and reflect on your days. This is about taking a couple of minutes at the end of your day and to take a look at what you did well, get some perspective, relive the happy moments and write everything down in your journal.

By doing this, you will receive an extra boost of happiness, motivation and self-esteem every morning and evening. It has the positive side effect that just before going to bed, you will be concentrating on positive things, which has a beneficial effect on your sleep and your subconscious mind. Your focus is on the positive things of the day and gratitude instead of the things that didn't work well, which probably would keep you awake, and by now you know how crucial that is! For my clients and also for myself, this little exercise has led to enormous changes in our well-being.

Make an effort to answer the following questions each night before going to bed and write them in your journal:

- What am I grateful for? (Write three to five points)
- Which three things have made me happy today?
- Which three things did I do particularly well today?
- How could I have made today even better?
- What is my most important goal for tomorrow?

Don't worry if the words don't flow right away when you start his exercise. Like all other things, your journaling will get better with practise. If you reach a dead end and can't think of anything, just hold on for five minutes longer. Write what comes to mind without thinking and don't judge it. Don't worry about your style or mistakes. Just write! Do this every day for a month and observe the changes that take place! A regular notebook or calendar should do. I'm using a lovely little book called "The Five-minute Journal".

65
Stop whining

Never tell your problems to anyone...
20% don't care and the other 80% are glad you have them.

—LOU HOLTZ

It is better to light a candle than to curse the darkness.

—CONFUCIUS

Complaining is poison in your desire to become happier.
It's an absolutely useless behavior that encourages self-pity and
doesn't accomplish anything. Complainers are not attractive at
all. It's the mentality of a victim and that isn't you any more,
is it? **Stop cursing the darkness and light a candle.** Stop
complaining about not having time and get up an hour earlier
(see Chapter 25). Stop complaining about your weight and start
exercising (see Chapter 75). Stop blaming your parents, your
teachers, your boss, the government or the economy, and take
responsibility for your life (see Chapter 3).

It's nobody's fault but your own that you cannot quit
smoking, that you eat unhealthy food or that you gave up on

your dream. It's you who pushes the snooze button instead of getting up half an hour earlier and who chooses fear over risk. Don't blame others for not living a satisfying life. You own your life! You can do anything you want with it. The sooner you get this, the sooner you can move on in the direction of your dreams. Remember where to keep your focus. Complaining about your present circumstances will put your focus on them and attract more of what you don't like. You have to get out of this vicious circle and concentrate on what you want instead (see Chapter 12).

Look inside yourself, encourage your positive ambitions and your will to succeed. Now go and create the circumstances you want. Start taking decisions and start living.

Action Steps:

1) Make a list of all your complaints.
2) What have you achieved through your complaints?
3) Transform your complaints into requests.

66

Become a receiver

I can live for two months on a good compliment.

—MARK TWAIN

Do you find it difficult to accept a gift or a compliment? Well, this stops NOW! You have to become a receiver! It's very important to accept gifts and things with joy and it's also the secret to getting more of what you want. If you get a present and you say, "Oh! That's not necessary," you are taking away the joy of giving a gift from the other person, and the same thing goes for compliments. **Take a closer look at this behavior!** Is there a hidden feeling of "I don't deserve this", or "I'm not worth it" behind the "That's not necessary?" There is no need for justification. Don't diminish the pleasure of giving for the other person. Just say "Thank you!" From today on, I dare you to practise your "receiving skills". If somebody gives you a compliment, accept it graciously with a "Thank you". Own it. Don't return it. You may say: "Thank you! I'm happy you feel that way!" and let the other person enjoy the experience. It will help you a lot and take your self-esteem to a whole new level if you manage to eradicate the following behaviors:

- Rejecting compliments.
- Belittling yourself.
- Giving credit to others although you have earned it.
- Not buying something nice because you think you don't deserve it.
- Looking for the negative if someone does something good for you.

Action Steps:

1) From now on, just say "Thank you!" for every gift and compliment you receive! (Don't explain or justify it)
2) Analyze if you have any of the five behaviors mentioned above. If yes, work on it/them.

67

Stop spending time with the wrong people

Whatever you do, you need courage.
Whatever course you decide upon, there will always be
someone to tell you that you are wrong.

—RALPH WALDO EMERSON

The person who says it can't be done shouldn't
interrupt the person who is doing it!

—CHINESE PROVERB

WATCH WHO YOU ARE SPENDING YOUR TIME WITH! Jim Rohn said that, "You are the average of the five persons you spend the most time with," so you better take this seriously. Choose to spend more time with people who bring out the best in you, who motivate you, who believe in you. Be around people who empower you. **Remember that emotions and attitudes are contagious.** People around you can be the springboard to motivate yourself, gain courage and help you take the right actions, but on the other hand, can also drag you down, drain your energy and act as brakes in the achieving of your life goals.

If you are around negative people all the time, they can convert you into a negative and cynical person over time. They might want to convince you to stay where you are and keep you stuck, because they value security and don't like risk and uncertainty. So **stay away from the naysayers**, **the blamers, the complainers.** The people who are always judging or gossiping and talking bad about everything. And as Steve Jobs said at the famous Stanford address, **"Don't let the noise of others' opinions drown your own inner voice."**

It will be difficult for you to grow and thrive, if people around you want to convince you of the contrary. And what do you do if it's people close to you? The only thing you can work on is becoming a better person yourself. If you grow and develop, soon negative people will turn away from you because you don't serve their purposes any more. They need somebody who shares their negativity and if you don't do that, they will look for somebody else. If that doesn't work, you seriously have to ask yourself the question if you should start to spend less time with them or stop seeing them at all. **But that's a decision you have to make.** In my whole life, I automatically separated people from my life that didn't support me and I never regretted it, although it wasn't easy! After my own coaching training—when I reinforced all the principles that you are learning in this book and changed myself—some of my colleagues had no other explanation than actually thinking that I had joined a sect.

Action Steps:

1. Make a list of all the people you have in your life and are spending time with. (Members of your family, friends, classmates, colleagues).
2. Analyze who is positive for you and who drags you down.
3. Spend more time with the positive people and stop seeing the toxic people (blamers, complainers) in your life, or at least spend less time with them.
4. Choose to be around positive people who support you.
5. Watch Steve Jobs' Stanford commencement address.

68
Live your own life

Your time is limited, so don't waste it living someone else's life.

Don't be trapped by dogma, which is living with the results of other people's thinking. Don't let the noise of others' opinions drown out your own inner voice.

And most important, have the courage to follow your heart and intuition.

They somehow already know what you truly want to become.

Everything else is secondary.

—STEVE JOBS

Actually this quote of Steve Jobs says everything! It's difficult to add something to his wise words. **Live the life you want and not the life other people expect of you.** Don't worry about what your neighbors or other people think of you, because if you care too much about what they say, there will be a moment when you don't live your own life any more, but the life of other people. Listen to your heart. Do the things you want to do, and not necessarily those things that everybody else does. Have the courage to be different! Paulo Coelho reminds us, "If someone isn't what others want them to be, the others become angry. Everyone seems to have a clear idea of how other people should lead their lives, but none about his or her own."

Action Step:

In what aspect are you not living your life right now? Make a list!

69

Who is number one?

No one can make you feel inferior without your consent.

—ELEANOR ROOSEVELT

Love yourself like your neighbor! Many times, you see the good in others and fail to see it in yourself! The most important relationship that you have in this life is the one you have with yourself! If you don't like yourself, how can you expect others to like you? How can you expect to love others, if you don't love yourself first?

We are going to work on your most important relationship. Most of the problems my clients come to me for depend directly or indirectly on self-confidence. The salary raise they don't get, the appreciation they don't get, the relationship they don't find. So I usually work with them on their self-confidence while working toward their goal. How do you gain more self-confidence? First of all, **accept yourself as you are.** You don't have to be perfect to be great! **Learn to spend time with the most important person in your life—YOU. Enjoy going to the movies with the best company you can imagine: YOU!** French writer and philosopher Blaise Pascal says, "All of humanity's problems stem from *man's* inability to *sit* quietly in a *room alone.*" Dr Wayne Dyer adds, "You cannot be lonely if you like the person you're alone with."

Get comfortable with spending some alone time. Find a place where you can disconnect from the speedy everyday life. It can't be mentioned often enough: **Accepting yourself is a key element of your well-being.** Recognize your value as a person. Know that you earn respect. If you make a mistake, don't beat yourself up over it, accept it and promise yourself to do your best to not repeat it. That's it. There is absolutely no use in beating yourself up about something that you can't change.

Be selfish! What? What am I saying? Yes, you read it right: Be selfish! I don't mean in an egocentric way, but by being well within yourself, so that you can transmit this wellness to your whole environment. If you are not well within yourself, you can't be a good husband, wife, son, daughter or friend. But if you feel great, you can transmit these feelings to your whole environment and everybody benefits. **Exercises to boost your self-confidence:**

1) The Journaling Exercise from Chapter 64
2) Make a list of your successes and achievements.
3) Make a list of all of the things you are doing great.
4) Mirror exercise (Tell yourself how great you are in front of a mirror! It may feel strange at first, but you'll get used to it).
5) Increase somebody else's self-esteem.

70
Your best investment

An investment in knowledge pays the best interest.

—BENJAMIN FRANKLIN

If you think education is expensive, try ignorance.

—DEREK BOK

The best thing you can do for your further personal and professional growth is to invest in yourself. Commit yourself to becoming the best person you can be. Invest around 5–10% of your income in training, books, CDs and other ways of personal development. Stay curious and eager to learn new things and better yourself. A positive side effect of investing in your personal growth is that while you become a wiser person, you might also become more valuable for your company. There are so many possibilities: you could learn training that improves your negotiating skills, time management, financial planning and much more. In a two- or four-hour workshop, you can learn powerful strategies or tools that can transform your life. Or you can decide to go all in and get a life coach and really start working on yourself. One of my best investments in myself ever was hiring a coach. He helped me to get unstuck, get clear about what I really want from my life and change my relationship with fear completely. You can also start in a less expensive way by reading more or listening to a learning CD or a course. I made it a habit to read at least one book a week, buy a new course every two months and sign up for at least two seminars or trainings a year.

What are you going to do? Remember that baby steps count, too!

Action Step:

Write down what you will commit to in the next 12 months: I, —— will read —— book(s) a month, listen to —— learning CDs or audiobooks per month, sign up for —— training(s) in the next six months.

Date: —————— Signature
: ——————

71

Stop being so hard on yourself

Because one believes in oneself,
one doesn't try to convince others.

Because one is content with oneself,
one doesn't need others' approval.

Because one accepts oneself, the whole
world accepts him or her.

—LAO TZU

It's easy to fall into the habit of self-criticism because of past mistakes or because things didn't work out as we wanted them to. But does it serve you? No, NADA, zip!

It's time you accept something here: You are not perfect! You never will be, and—the best thing is—YOU DON'T HAVE TO BE! So once and for all, stop being so hard on yourself! This is one of the top reasons that prevent people from living a happy and fulfilled life. Did you know that a lot of the misery we have in our life is because we subconsciously think we have to punish ourselves for something? I'm glad I left the habit of exaggerated self-criticism and self-punishment behind a long time ago. **I'm just conscious that I'm doing the best that I can at any time.** That doesn't mean I don't analyze the many mistakes I made. If I can correct them, I do; if I can't correct them, I accept them, let go and promise myself not to repeat them, because I know **it's only a problem if I keep repeating the same mistakes over and over again.** Is that too difficult? Do you want to know the magic recipe? It's not for sale in any pharmacy and it's free! Ready?

1) **Accept yourself as you are!**
2) **Forgive yourself! Love yourself!**
3) **Take extremely good care of yourself!** (see Chapter 73)

That's it! Easy, isn't it? **Start NOW!**

Ask yourself the following questions:

In what areas of your life are you being too hard on yourself?
What benefits do you get from being too hard on yourself?

72

Be your authentic self

We have to dare to be ourselves, however frightening
or strange that self may prove to be.

—MAY SARTON

To be yourself in a world that is constantly trying to make you
something else is the greatest accomplishment.

—RALPH WALDO EMERSON

The most successful people are the ones who are authentic. They are not playing any roles. They are who they are. What you see is what you get! They know their strengths and their weaknesses. They have no problem in being vulnerable and taking responsibility for their mistakes. Neither do they fear judgment of others. **Don't let the world tell you who you are supposed to be.** Your fake self is who you are when you want to please everyone else. That's when you have a mask on and are keen to get feedback from the people who surround you such as colleagues, friends, neighbors, etc. **Don't play any roles!** Stop thinking about what others want of you, or might think of

you, and **give yourself permission to be your authentic self.**
The rewards are awesome! Funnily enough, you will notice that
the more you are yourself, the more people will be attracted
to you! Try it out!

Questions:

1) On a scale of 0–10, how would you quantify your level of
    authenticity?
    An eight? Congratulations! You are quite close. Keep on
    improving!
    A four? Well there is some work to do, but going through
    the exercises in this book you will help you get closer!
2) How many roles do you play?
3) Who are you when you are alone?
4) When was the last time you felt authentic?

73

Pamper yourself

*You can change the way people treat you
by changing the way you treat yourself.*

—UNKNOWN

This is one of my favorite exercises for my clients! Write down
a list of 15 things that you can do to pamper yourself and then
do one of them every other day for the next two weeks. This
exercise is truly miraculous! (Examples: read a good book, go
to the movies, get a massage, watch a sunrise, sit by the water,
etc.) Once you start treating yourself well, it **will do miracles
for your self-confidence and self-esteem! Start doing it NOW!**

1. _____
2. _____
3. _____
4. _____
5. _____
6. _____
7. _____
8. _____

9. _____
10. _____
11. _____
12. _____
13. _____
14. _____
15. _____

74

Treat your body like the temple it is

*To keep the body in good health is a duty, otherwise
we shall not be able to keep our mind strong and clear.*

—BUDDHA

Isn't it ironic? If you listen to people, most of us say that health
is the most important thing in our lives; nevertheless many people
drink, smoke, eat junk food or even take drugs, and spend most
of their free time on the couch without any physical activity.
Remember—it's easy! **A healthier life is only a decision away.**
Decide NOW to live healthier. Follow a **balanced diet, exercise
regularly** and **stay or get in shape,** so that your brain has all
the nutrition it needs to produce a positive lifestyle. Take care
of your body, because if the body is not well, the mind doesn't
work well either. Here are some examples:

- Eat more fruit and vegetables.
- Reduce your intake of red meat.
- Drink at least two liters of water each day.
- Eat less!
- Stop eating junk food.

- Get up early.

Action Steps:

What will you do now for a healthier lifestyle?

Write down at least three things:

_____

_____

_____

_____

_____

75

Exercise at least three times a week

*Those who do not find time for exercise
will have to find time for illness.*

—EDWARD SMITH-STANLEY

I think I'm not coming to you with breaking news here if I tell you how important exercise is for you. And even if we all know about the importance of exercise, there are many of us who just don't do it. The most common excuse is: "I have no time." But what if somebody were to tell you that your life depends on it? And if you don't start exercising right now, you will be dead in a month? You will surely find time, wouldn't you? So time is not the problem. I also won't put a lot of work into convincing you how important exercise is and how you can find time, because you already know that. I will just list the benefits of exercising three to five times a week. And then—if you want—you will find the time.

1. Exercising will keep you healthy.
2. Exercising will help you lose weight, which will improve your health and also make you look better.

3. Exercising will make you feel better and you will have a lot of energy.
4. Once the kilos start dropping, there is a big chance that your self-esteem will go up. I can confirm that.
5. Problems with falling asleep? Exercise for 30 minutes a couple of hours before you go to sleep and see what it does for you.
6. Have you ever noticed that exercise significantly reduces stress? First of all there are the endorphins, but the other thing is that you just might get your mind off the things that were stressing you out.

Furthermore, studies show that regular exercise makes you happier, reduces the symptoms of depression and the risk of diseases (heart diseases, diabetes, osteoporosis, high cholesterol, among others.), lowers the risk of a premature death and improves your memory, and many more. Are you in?

One last thing: Don't force yourself to exercise. Enjoy it. Look for a recreational activity that fits you and that you enjoy doing such as swimming, for example. Even walking an hour a day can make a difference. (see Chapter 34)

Action steps:

1) Find some studies about the amazing benefits of exercise on the Internet.
2) When will YOU start exercising?
3) If you think you don't have time, go back to the Chapters about finding time.

76

Take action. Make things happen

Whatever you do, or dream you can, begin it.
Boldness has genius and power and magic in it.

—JOHANN WOLFGANG VON GOETHE

I am only one, but I am one.
I cannot do everything, but I can do something.

And I will not let what I cannot do
interfere with what I can do.

—EDWARD EVERETT HALE

One of the secrets to success and happiness in life is to make things happen. Just talking about it is not enough. It's the results that count or as Henry Ford said, **"You can't build a reputation on what you are going to do."** Without action, there are no results. Without results, there is no feedback. Without feedback, there is no learning. Without learning, we can't improve. Without improving, we can't develop our full potential.

C.G. Jung said it correctly, "You are what you do, not what

you say you'll do." **There are too many people who want to change the world yet never picked up a pen to start writing a book or an article or did anything about it.** It's a lot easier to complain about our politicians, than to start pursuing a political career or become more active in politics. Your life is in your hands, so start acting on your ideas. You don't have to go for the big challenges at once. By now, you have learned that doing small things consistently on a daily basis can get you great results. Dare to do the things you want and you will find the power to do them. **But by all means START NOW! The biggest difference between people who reach their goals and people who stay stuck is ACTION.** People who reach their goals are doers who are taking action consistently. If they make a mistake, they learn from it and move on; if they are rejected, they try again. **People who stay stuck just talk about what they are going to do and don't walk their talk.** Don't wait any longer! The right moment never comes! Just start with what you have and go one step at a time. Do as Martin Luther King, Jr. said, **"Take the first step in faith. You don't have to see the whole staircase, just take the first step."**

Action Step:

What will you start TODAY?

77

Enjoy more

The present moment is filled with joy and happiness.
If you are attentive, you will see it.

—THÍCH NHÂT HANH

Real generosity toward the future
lies in giving all to the present.

—ALBERT CAMUS

It's very important to enjoy the present moment! If you don't, then life goes by and you don't even notice it, because you are never right here, in the moment! When you're working, you think of the weekend, on the weekend, you think of all the things you have to do on Monday, when you're eating the appetizer, you think of dessert, and when you eating dessert, you think of the appetizer—with the result that you don't fully enjoy neither the one nor the other.

And living like this, you never get to enjoy your point of power, the only moment that counts—the present moment. Eckart Tolle wrote an entire book about "The power of NOW" which I highly recommend to you. Think about it: Do you have any problem RIGHT NOW just being in the moment? Do you constantly live with guilt for your past actions and with fear of an unknown future? Many people are constantly worrying about things in the past that they can't change or things in the future that—even funnier—mostly never happen, and meanwhile they miss out on the NOW or as Bill Cosby puts it, **"The past is a ghost, the future a dream. All we ever have is now."** Just be present and enjoy the journey.

Action Step:

Remind yourself to be more in the present moment!

(My friend David wears his wristwatch on his right arm. This reminds him to be in the present moment whenever he watches his left arm for the time and notices it's not there.)

78
Stop judging

Before you accuse me, take a look at yourself.

—ERIC CLAPTON

Before you start pointing fingers, make sure your hands are clean.

—BOB MARLEY

Judging goes hand in hand with the vices of blaming and complaining; on your way to a happier, more fulfilling life that's another bad habit you have to leave behind!

Accept others without judging them, and without expectations. I know that's easier said than done, but there is no way around it! **Think of it this way: each time you're judging somebody, you are actually judging yourself.** Isn't it true that the things that bother us the most about others are actually the things that bother us the most about ourselves?

Action Step:

Make a list of what bothers you the most about others.

79

A random act of kindness every day

*One of the most difficult things to give away
is kindness; usually it comes back to you.*

—ANONYMOUS

The smallest good deed is better than the grandest intention.

—ANONYMOUS

How can you make the world a little bit better today and every day? Why not be nice to a stranger every day? Be creative! Every now and then I pay for two coffees instead of the only one that I drank and tell the server to save it, in case somebody needs it and can't pay for it entirely. In the supermarket, if I get a 10% discount voucher for my next shopping trip, I usually give it to the person behind me in line. You can offer your seat in the train or subway to somebody or even just gift somebody with a smile. Acknowledge people sincerely, treat people great, say "thank you" genuinely, hold the door open for somebody, help somebody whose hands are full to carry something or store away somebody's heavy hand luggage on your next flight. Be creative! Start today! The great thing is: "What goes around comes around." So, when you start doing random acts of kindness, more kindness is coming back to you! Doing good begins to become the same thing as feeling good. The good that we do for others really does have the power to change us. **If you want to improve the world then start with yourself! Be the change you want to see in the world! Do at least ONE random act of kindness every day.** Positively and significantly impact the lives of other people. **PAY IT FORWARD!**

Action Step:

Commit yourself to doing one random act of kindness a day for the next two weeks.

Observe what happens, but don't expect anything in return!

80

Solve your problems, all of them

*Most people spend more time and energy going
around problems than in trying to solve them.*

—HENRY FORD

**Solve your problems. Face them. Because if you are running
away from them, they will come after you.** If you don't solve
them, they will repeat themselves over and over again until you
learn something and are ready to move on.

For example, if you change jobs because of problems with
a colleague that you didn't tackle, in another job, you may
face the same challenge with another person. This will go on
until you learn something out of the situation and solve the
problem once and for all. Did you notice that you may continue
to encounter the same set of problems in multiple romantic
relationships until you stop and solve the recurring problems?
Another giant waste of energy is to dance around problems
and responsibilities instead of somebody taking ownership and
starting to solve problems. I hear this over and over again from
my clients: they procrastinate, they dance around the problem

and end up with a high level of anxiety and feeling really bad. Once they decide to go against all their fears and confront and solve the problem, they feel much better and find out that it was a lot less painful to face the problem and solve it than the whole process of dancing around it. Stop searching for the solution to your problems "out there", and start looking for it within you.

Questions:

How can you be different? What can you do differently? What can YOU do to solve the problem?

Action step:

1) Make a list of all your problems and start working on their solutions.
2) Examine your problems and
3) Look for patterns (Do the same things happen to you over and over again?)

81

The power of meditation

All of humanity's problems stem from man's inability to sit quietly in a room alone.

—BLAISE PASCAL

The benefits of meditation are widely known by now. More and more people have started practising it. The practitioners of meditation highlight its usefulness in calming the mind after a stressful day, and in warding off anxiety, anger, insecurity and even depression. Other studies point out that meditation can reduce blood pressure and pain response. It's an easy way of stress combat and quieting our information-overloaded mind. Just sitting still for 15 to 20 minutes once a day can already make a difference and help you to recharge. If you do it twice a day...even better! Here is how to begin your habit of daily meditation:

1. Look for a space where you won't be disturbed and just be in silence for 15 to 20 minutes. Make it a ritual. It's beneficial to practise in the same spot and at the same time every day. Do you remember the magic of

the early-morning hours? Maybe that's also a good time for your meditation.

2. Before you start, use the power of affirmations to get yourself in a relaxed state by saying for example, "I'm now focused and calm."

3. Set your alarm clock for 20 minutes so that you are not worried about when to stop your meditation, and are fully able to concentrate.

4. Sit or lie down and shut your eyes. You can also leave your eyes open and focus on one point in the room or on nature if you are facing a window.

5. While focusing, concentrate on your breath and start relaxing.

6. When your mind wanders let it wander. Don't resist. See your thoughts passing by like clouds in the blue sky and just empty your mind. See your mind still like a lake without the smallest ripple.

Meditating for 20 minutes a day will surely provide you with great results once you have made it a habit. The six steps mentioned above are only a suggestion. **Meditation can't be done wrong and only you will know what works best for you.** There is also a lot of information on the Internet, as well as classes and seminars that may be available close to where you live. **The most important thing is—as everything in this book—TO TAKE ACTION! Try it out!**

82

Listen to great music—daily

Life is one grand, sweet song, so start the music.

—RONALD REAGAN

An easy way to feel happy instantly is to listen to your favorite music! Make a soundtrack of your all-time favorites and listen to them, dance to them and sing along! It might feel stupid at first, but doing this every day will be very beneficial.

What are your top five favorite songs of all time?

1. _____
2. _____
3. _____
4. _____
5. _____

Why not make a playlist on your iPod, phone or PC and listen to them right now! **Do it NOW! Come on!**

How did you feel after listening to your favorite song? **Any changes in your mood?**

What would happen if you made this a daily habit?

83
No worries

If a problem is fixable, if a situation is such
that you can do something about it,

Then there is no need to worry. If it's not fixable,
then there is no help in worrying.

There is no benefit in worrying whatsoever.

—DALAI LAMA XIV

Many people are constantly worrying. They worry about things that happened in the past that they can't change, about things in the future that they have no influence over, or about the economy, wars and politics which they have no control over. Even funnier is that most of the catastrophes that you are worrying about turn out to be a lot less horrible in reality or just never happen. Mark Twain was right when he said, **"I've had a lot of worries in my life, most of which never happened."**

Keep in mind: it doesn't matter how much you worry, it will change neither the past, nor the future! Also, worrying usually doesn't make things any better, does it? Instead, it will drag you down and you will lose the present moment. Can you already grasp what a waste of time and energy worrying is or shall I give you another example? This example is from Robin Sharma's book "Who Will Cry When You Die?" A Manager who did one of the exercises Robin suggests at his seminars identified the following: 54% of his worries were about things that would probably never happen; 26% were related to past actions that couldn't be changed; 8% were related to other people's opinions which he didn't even care about; 4% were personal health questions that he had already resolved. **Only 8% referred to questions that needed his attention.** Identifying his problems and dropping the ones he couldn't do anything about or which were just draining energy, the man eliminated 92% of the worries that had tortured him so much.

Action step:

Make a list of your worries.

Which ones are related to the past?

Which ones are related to the future?

Which ones are outside your control?

Which ones can you actually do something about?

84

Use your travel time wisely

Time is what we want most, but what we use worst.

—WILLIAM PENN

How much time are you spending every day in the car or public transport on your way to work? Statistics say it's between 60 and 90 minutes per working day! That means, in a month we are taking between 20 to 30 hours. Who says, "I don't have enough time ?" We just found you another 20 to 30 hours to read (when on a bus or train), or listen to audio books in your car. What if you really spent that time listening to empowering CDs, mp3s or reading inspirational books instead of listening to the negative news on the radio or reading about it in the newspaper?

Questions:

Are you ready to try it out?

When will you start?

Do it for two weeks and let me know how your life changed.

85

Spend more time with your family

Family is not an important thing, it's everything.

—MICHAEL J. FOX

Walt Disney once said, "A man should never neglect his family for business." Yet I have to dedicate an extra chapter to this one. **Just to make sure that you don't skip it!** It's kind of sad that I have to mention it, but when I interview leaders and executives, most of the time what comes up is that they just cannot (?) spend a lot of time with their families!

In Bronnie Ware's book "The Top Five Regrets of the Dying: A Life Transformed by the Dearly Departing" (see also Chapter 94), one of the top regrets of the dying is to not have spent more time with their families and having spent too much time at the office! Don't become one of them and **start making time for your family NOW!** And if you are with the family…do everybody a favor and BE FULLY with the family.

During our vacation in the Florida Keys last year, I saw an absurd situation. A family was on a sightseeing walk with the father running ahead in the front making a business phone call, while the wife and daughter were following looking kind of sad, which is understandable. It was even a Sunday! It seemed like something taken out of a comic book, and yet it was very real and sad to see. **WAKE UP!** Value your family and friends. They are your constant source of love and mutual support, which increases your self-esteem and boosts your self-confidence.

Questions:

How are you going to find more time for your family? (Tip: Use the Time Management tips in this book) What will you stop doing to find more time?

86

Don't be the slave of your phone

Men have become the tools of their tool.

—HENRY DAVID THOREAU

Going back to the busy father mentioned in the last chapter, this tip comes in handy. **Don't always pick up your phone each time it rings;** your phone is supposed to be for YOUR convenience, not for those who call you. Give yourself the freedom to continue what you are doing and let the call go to voice mail. Some time ago, I always got very anxious when I didn't take a call. **I thought I had missed something.** My roommate Pol was much cooler about it. He only answered the phone when he wanted to, when he felt like it, and if not—he just went on doing what he was doing without bothering. I started liking the idea and worked on adapting this "Zen-like" mentality, telling myself that, "They will call again." I also learnt that if it's a really important call, the caller will not give up and probably call five times within three minutes.

Action Step:

Try it out! Don't be a slave of your phone and leverage voicemail.

87

How to deal with problems

Every problem has in it the seeds of its own solution.
If you don't have any problems, you don't get any seeds.

—NORMAN VINCENT PEALE

Do you have many problems? Congratulations!!! And I'm not kidding! You have many opportunities to grow, because a problem is always an opportunity to grow by learning from it! So, let's have a better look at this. Over 20 years ago, when I started working at Disneyworld in Orlando, we—the newbies—were taught that the word "problem" doesn't exist in the vocabulary of a Disney Cast Member: "We don't have problems, we only have **challenges** here." Dr Lair Ribeiro writes that, "Your problems are your best friends" and Leadership Guru Robin Sharma asks us to see our problems as blessings! So what are problems now? Challenges, blessings, friends? Or all three of them? Isn't life just about facing one problem after another? What makes all the difference is how you face it and how you learn from it! When you start learning from your problems, life gets much better. Look back at the problems you had in your life. Didn't each one of it have something positive?

Maybe a loss in business saved you from an even bigger loss, because you learnt from it. In hard times, it can be very beneficial for you to adapt the belief that life/God/the universe only puts a problem in your way if you are able to solve it!

Questions:

1) What problems do you have in your life right now that you haven't found a solution for yet?
2) Make a list of your problems.
3) What would change if you see these problems as challenges or even opportunities? How would it make you feel?

88

Take time off

There is more to life than increasing its speed.

—MAHATMA GANDHI

With the stressful, fast-paced life that we are living, it becomes even more important to slow down our pace of life and take a break! Take some time off. Recharge your batteries by being around nature. You can start by scheduling some relaxation time into your weekly planner, which by now you are hopefully making time for (see Chapter 22).

If you dare, start with weekends in which you are completely disconnected from the Internet, TV and your electronic games. One of my best vacations ever—if not the best—was being on a houseboat in the Midi Channel in the south of France. No mobile phone, no Internet, no TV. Only ducks. The boat's top speed was 8 km/hr (= 5 miles/hr), so we were literally "forced" to slow down. It is also due to the fact that when you are floating on the channel, children on their bikes overtake you on one side of the channel. The villages you pass through are sometimes so small, that they don't even have a supermarket.

So the whole trip comes down to the question, "Where will we get food?" No worries! There is always a restaurant close by, but the charming thing is to cook your own meals on the boat and have dinner at the harbor watching the sunset or just being around nature. Once, we had dinner in the middle of a vineyard! Priceless! So is to walk into a tiny French village in the morning and get your baguette for breakfast from the only bakery in town. We got up at sunrise and went to bed two chess matches after sunset. Or as we described it afterwards, "We got up with the ducks and went to sleep with the ducks."

Take time off and connect with nature! It doesn't have to be a long trip. Walk in the woods, on the beach or in a park whenever you get the chance and observe how you feel afterwards. Or just lie down on a bench or in the grass and contemplate the blue sky. When was the last time you walked barefoot on grass or on a beach? Did you get the idea of how important, relaxing and reenergizing taking some time off is for you? I hope so! **What will you do?**

Action Step:

Schedule some relaxation time in your calendar right now!

89

Have a highlight every day

I believe the key to happiness is someone to love,
something to do, and something to look forward to.

—ELVIS PRESLEY

Don't let routine and boredom crawl into your life. Create
things you look forward to after a hard day at work instead
of just ending up in front of the TV every evening. Here are
some examples:

- Take some "alone time".
- Go for a walk in the nature with your spouse.
- Take a bubble bath or have a spa day.
- Celebrate something: a good job, family, life!
- Call a friend.
- Take somebody for lunch.
- Get a massage.
- Go for a drink.
- Go to the movies/theater/a concert.
- Get a manicure/pedicure.
- Indulge in a movie night at home.

- Watch a sunrise, etc.

Remember to reserve some time for your special moments in your schedule!

90

Step out of your "comfort zone"

As you move outside of your comfort zone, what was once the unknown and frightening becomes your new normal.

—ROBIN SHARMA

One can choose to go back toward safety or forward toward growth. Growth must be chosen again and again; fear must be overcome again and again.

—ABRAHAM MASLOW

Have you ever heard of the saying, "The magic happens outside of your comfort zone?"

But...what the heck is the comfort zone? The following metaphor describes it very well: if you put a frog into a pot of boiling water, it jumps out! But if you put it into a pot and start heating up the water gradually, it doesn't react and dies by being boiled! And that's what happens to many people who are trapped in their comfort zone without even knowing it.

Your comfort zone is the limit of your current experience.

It's what you are used to doing, thinking or feeling based on your current level of knowledge. It's where it's nice and cozy, and where we know most of the time exactly what is going to happen. It's where you live life on autopilot. It's also where change doesn't happen.

Personal growth and development happen outside of your comfort zone. So, if you want to change jobs, start an enterprise, be creative, get out of a relationship that has stopped working, you have to step out of your comfort zone. Unfortunately it's more comfortable to stay where you are and your mind is doing everything to keep you there! When I was trapped in a job that I didn't like any more, I caught myself saying the entire time, "Well, it's not that bad, it could be worse. Who knows, maybe in another job I would be even worse off." And so I continued in a job that no more made sense to me day in day out. One Monday, I was already looking forward to Friday, and when I came back from my vacation, I was already looking to the next one. Can you imagine that? I should have watched Steve Jobs' commencement Address at Stanford some years earlier. (**Did you watch it yet?**)

Jobs had a great technique: each day he looked at himself in the mirror and asked, "If today were the last day of my life, would I want to do what I'm about to do today?" and if he answered "No" to himself for too many days in a row, he changed!

Be careful if you use that technique, **because once you start asking yourself this question everything changes.** When you step out of your comfort zone and start to venture toward the unknown, you start to grow. **You will start feeling uncomfortable and awkward. That's a great sign! That's actually a sign that you are growing and moving ahead.** Act in spite of fear and doubt!

Questions:

1) How can you challenge yourself to step out of your comfort zone? (Remember, small steps!)
2) Is there anything that makes you uncomfortable that you can do NOW?

91

What price are you paying for NOT changing?

The price of doing the same old thing is far higher than the price of change.

—BILL CLINTON

Another question that forced me out of my comfort zone when I was evaluating my situation was, **"What is the price you are paying for not taking action?"** I was on the worst possible way to being seriously burnt out. Of course, it was very risky to just walk away from my secure job without putting up a fight in the worst economic crisis the world had seen, but what was the price I was paying to stay? Serious health problems? No thanks, buddy! I'm out of here. Since then, I never looked back.

Many years ago, my boss at Volkswagen in Mexico came to me—the intern—and said, "Marc, I don't know what to do any more. I'm close to a breakdown due to stress, but I'm on a three-year Expat-contract and if I break it, I will be looked at as a failure at the headquarters in Germany. What would you do?" I told him,

202 • Marc Reklau

Look, your health is the most important thing you have. If this job affects your health any more, leave. Because if you get a heart attack and die, the people that are now giving you the worst time will say what a great guy you were at your funeral in front of your wife and kid. I'm talking from my own personal experience: the people that harassed my father the most at his work, actually wanted to speak at his funeral! Unbelievable! For now, I would hang in there and see what happens, because I really believe that life is a miracle, everything happens for a reason and in the end everything is always going to work out!

Two months later, he contacted me from Germany. He was still on his Expat-contract, however he had returned to Germany and was working on a new project with far better work conditions. Life is a miracle—it always works out in the end! **But there is always a price you are paying and it's your decision if you want to pay it and live with the consequences.** The price you pay if you want to get in shape is that you have to exercise. The price you pay for not exercising is getting overweight. If you want more time the price is getting up an hour earlier or watching less TV. The price you pay for procrastination is facing anxiety and feeling bad. **Choose your suffering wisely!**

Question:

1) Are you paying a price for doing the same old thing?

92

Things are only temporary

You can't connect the dots looking forward; you can only connect them looking backwards. So you have to trust that the dots will somehow connect in your future.

—STEVE JOBS

It does not matter how slowly you go as long as you do not stop.

—CONFUCIUS

Everything is temporary. All triumphs, defeat, joy, sadness that happen in our life go by. What seems to be very important today might not be important any more in a month or three months. **And what seems to be a disaster today can be a great learning experience three months from now.** When I was jobless for over nine months right after finishing college and was rejected by, I don't even remember how many companies, each one of my friends was pitying me and most of all, I pitied myself. But somehow, deep down inside, I knew that **all of the rejection is because something better is waiting** for me. In the end, I started working in Barcelona, one of the most beautiful cities in the world with lots of culture, beaches, a fantastic climate, a great football team, and about 300 days of sun a year (very important for me at that time). My friends went directly from pity to envy and from "poor Marc" to "lucky bastard!"

Look at life with a little more ease and sobriety knowing that misfortunes pass. Or as Rudyard Kipling in his fantastic poem "If" says, **"If you can meet with Triumph and Disaster and treat those two impostors just the same; [...] yours is the Earth and everything that's in it, And—which is more—you'll be a Man, my son!"**

Keep your attention on what you want and keep moving forward. Do you remember the saying, "In six months we are going to laugh about it!"? **Why not laugh already now?** This phrase actually got me through my International Business studies. I remember many nights before the exams at 3 a.m.—a few hours before the exam—when I was totally stressed out in the dorm room of my friend Jorge and on the verge of a breakdown (failing those exams would have meant dropping out of college or worse still... be thrown out) and he always just laughed and said, **"Marc, in six months we are going to laugh about tonight!"** We actually even now—20 years later—still laugh about those stories. Try this technique! I hope it helps you as it helped me!

Action Steps:

1. Think back on other hard times in your life and how you got out of it and maybe even found something positive in it after some time.

MAPPING LIFE:

1. Make a timeline of your life—from birth until now. Mark every key event in your life on the line. All and any moments that changed your life.
2. Write down the great moments, the successes above the timeline.
3. Write down the challenges, the tragedies, the failures below the timeline.
4. Examine the events below the line and write the positive effects of them above the line.

   (For example, somebody close to you died. A positive could be that you value your life more. Or perhaps you got fired from a job. This opened doors to an even better job that you have now.)

93
Get a coach

Make the most of yourself....for that is all there is of you.

—RALPH WALDO EMERSON

After having a huge impact in business life, coaching is also becoming more and more available for private persons in the form of life coaching. Many people have the wrong concept that you only take on a coach when something is wrong, but people like Eric Schmidt actually take on coaches to get even better, or to have a neutral, objective partner with whom they can bounce back and forth their ideas and who keeps them grounded.

A coach can help you to achieve clarity on what you really want in life, encourage you to keep on going when you would normally stop, help set better and more rewarding goals for yourself, get results more easily and quickly, overcome fear, communicate much more effectively, experience a faster personal development, overcome self-sabotaging habits, find your true purpose and to live aligned with your true values.

During the coaching process, you will learn to take

responsibility for everything in your life and take better decisions. Coaching achieves extraordinary results because you and your coach become a team, focusing on your goals and accomplishing more than you could do alone. You take more action, think bigger, and get the job done, because of the accountability the coach provides. A coach knows how to help you to make better decisions, set the best goals and restructure your professional and personal life for maximum productivity. Coaching works because it brings out the best in you. A coach is trained to help you find your own best answers and will support you in the course of that process. Coaching is usually done during regular, weekly sessions by telephone, skype or in person which last between 30 and 60 minutes. In every session coach and coachee work on the coachee's goals, creating options and setting a plan of action for the coachee's next steps. While working toward the coachee's goal, the coach also works on the coachee's personal development. You can find coaches, for example, in online directories of Coach U or the International Coach Federation (ICF). Most coaches offer complementary strategy sessions. That's how you and your coach get to know each other and find out if you are comfortable working together. Chemistry is crucial in a coaching relationship. **There is no guarantee that coaching works. Your success depends on you!** From my experience, I can say that the coaches who regularly attend their sessions, are committed to their coaching process and do their work end up being successful in their endeavors. That's why I even offer a 30-day money back guarantee (based on some ground rules).

94

Live your life fully. Do it NOW

Do not dwell in the past, do not dream of the future,
concentrate the mind on the present moment.

—BUDDHA

Most of us live like we have all the time in the world! We are so busy going after the big pleasures of life that we forget about the small ones. When will you start to take better care of yourself, start exercising, learn something new, do the things you always wanted to do, spend more time with your family? Tomorrow? Next week? Next Monday? Next month? When you win the lottery? When you have another job? When the next project is finished? Yes, I know. There are so many other things you have to do right now. You just don't have time right now! A lot of people never discover the meaning of life until it's too late and they are just about to die. Bronnie Ware, an Australian nurse who accompanied the dying, wrote down their top five regrets:

1. I wish I'd had the courage to live a life true to myself, not the life others expected of me.

2. I wish I didn't work so hard.
3. I wish I'd had the courage to express my feelings.
4. I wish I had stayed in touch with my friends.
5. I wish that I had let myself be happier.

Don't wait any longer. Live your life fully. NOW! Remember that failure is only feedback, that problems are opportunities to grow. Do the things you always wanted to do. Don't postpone them any longer. Don't fight life! Let it flow, because as Paulo Coelho says, **"One day you will wake up and there won't be any *more time* to do the things you've always wanted to do. Do it now."**

Steve Jobs put it this way:

Remembering that I'll be dead soon is the most important tool I've ever encountered to help me make the big choices in life. Almost everything—all external expectations, all pride, all fear of embarrassment or failure—these things just fall away in the face of death, leaving only what is truly important. Remembering that you are going to die is the best way I know to avoid the trap of thinking you have something to lose. You are already naked. There is no reason not to follow your heart. No one wants to die. Even people who want to go to heaven don't want to die to get there. And yet, death is the destination we all share. No one has ever escaped it, and that is how it should be, because death is very likely the single best invention of life. It's life's change agent. It clears out the old to make way for the new.

Every day brings with it opportunities to move closer to what you want, every day contributes to the end result. Don't let these opportunities pass. **It doesn't take months or years to change** your life; you change it step by step, day by day—starting NOW! The results, however, you will see for months and years.

Do yourself a favor and START LIVING NOW: not after the kids are out of the house, after you have finished the next project, after you have got the new car, after you have moved to the new house or after you have got a better job. Don't be one of those people who say they don't have time but spend 30 hours a week in front of the TV, playing video games or going out drinking.

Do the things you always wanted to do NOW. Make plans NOW!

List five things you always wanted to do and set a date:

1. ———————————— Date: —————
2. ———————————— Date: —————
3. ———————————— Date: —————
4. ———————————— Date: —————
5. ———————————— Date: —————

One last thing...

If you have been inspired by "30 Days" and want to help others to reach their goals and improve their lives, here are some action steps you can take immediately to make a positive difference:

Gift "30 Days: Change your habits change your life" to friends, family, colleagues and even strangers, so that they can also learn how to reach their goals and live great lives.

Please share your thoughts about this book on Twitter, Facebook and Instagram or write a book review. It helps other people find "30 Days".

If you own a business or if you are a manager—or even if you're not—gift some copies to your team or employees and improve the productivity of your company.

If you have a Podcast or know somebody that has one, ask them to interview me. I'm always happy to spread the message of "30 Days" and help people improve their lives.

Acknowledgements

Thanks to my father (R.I.P.), who in his very own way helped me become the person I am today. My mother Heidi for handing me the book that changed my life about 25 years ago, teaching me values and letting me go without any emotional blackmailing when I had to follow my heart for the first time and every time thereafter. My granny, for being one of my best buddies and providing retreat when I needed it. My cousin Alexander Reklau, who—when we were 16 years old—spoke very wise words which became part of my life story and probably saved me: "My father did with his life what he wanted; I will do with my life what I want!" I picked these words up two years later, after burying my father, and decided to live by them ever since.

My friends Pol and Inma for letting me stay at their house on the beautiful Island of Ibiza. A wonderful place to get the creative juices flowing.

My editor Gisela who helped me fine-tune the book.

My friend and mentor Stefan Ludwig, who provided me with his advice for over 10 years now. My friend Claudio, for always being there. Sabrina Kraus, Mari Arveheim and Marc Serrano Ossul, for their feedback during the writing process. My own coach Josep Anguera, who with his skills helped me to get unstuck after five years of stagnation. Talane Miedaner, whose book "Coach yourself to success" was my first contact with coaching and applying some of the tips she suggested changed my life dramatically.

Thank you to all of my clients for trusting me, letting me be a part of your enormous growth and allowing me the opportunity to grow with you all.

Last but not least, thanks to everybody I met along the way. You were either a friend or a teacher, or both!